the unknowed things

other books by Sean Brijbasi

One Note Symphonies
for Emma

Still Life in Motion
for those who play
Marius and Andréus

the unknowed things

Pretend Genius Press
London, New York, San Francisco, Seattle, Washington D.C.

www.pretendgenius.com

Published simultaneously in the United States and Great Britain in 2009
by Pretend Genius Press

Copyright © Sean Brijbasi

ISBN 978-0-9778526-0-4

Thanks to

Adrian
Nadira
Helena
Elijah
William
Olivia

(and
of
course
Mom
and
Dad)

Contents

for Julius

'Are we not weary men Caesar?'

'Not so weary that we cannot find our rest in chaos.'

god 23 (she)

god 23 (she)

I remember remembering—as I stood on the train platform, waiting for the train that would take me to Prague and my new life as fifth violin for the Czech Symphony Orchestra—of an advertisement I placed in Le Monde, looking for a woman (of rare beauty) who, unfortunately, had but one arm. I remember remembering that I had never seen such a woman but that I was searching, curious to know that if in all of Paris, in that great and teeming metropolis, such a woman existed.

I don't remember remembering Anna but I would like to, so that next time I remember remembering, she is placed in that memory as if she were always there. Of how I looked down to the tracks and thought of her irrational death and of how it related to my search for a woman with one arm (of rare beauty), whose name I wished 'with all my heart' to be Helen. So that next time, perhaps on my return to Paris, I shall say to the person sitting beside me:

In the belly of Les Halles I stood, waiting for the train to Prague, remembering the advertisement I placed in Le Monde, looking for a woman (of rare beauty), who, unfortunately, had but one arm, when the image of Anna standing where I stood came to me. I imagined watching her as I descended the stairs and of how she looked to the right and then to the left and as the train moved into the station, she threw herself in front of it without a fuss and died violently.

Irrational because of its apparent discontext in the grandeur of an escaping universe—a capitulation to the *disjecta merabra* of trace concepts regarding false notions of Helen, Anna, and that famous matador, Nathan. The woman with one arm, comprised of a combination of two odes. The first, a blacksmith's tale. The second, a lament on the death of the aforementioned matador who turned his back and lowered his head (as if the woman he loved danced too intimately with another man) and was lifted to the sun. A slow and sagging *parapluie* as the audience watched from beneath their hats, raised their arms, and made circles with their fingers (in that moist air my friends) to tell the bull *comenzar*.

The matador fell (silently) and blossoms thrown but not this blossom that was so unaffected by the wind and that, in turn, turned into a *blossoom*, unplucked until plucked by me, a gift for my Helen should I ever find her. One lonely *blossoom* growing atop the coliseum from where I searched the city while all manner of cape undulated behind me.

Oh Helen, I shall find you. I shall find you and give you this *blossoom*. But he who sat beside me on my trip to Prague stumbled in his understanding of my remembrance and in the convention of all that was modern I explained the symbolism behind my remembrance and that in lieu of *vocabulaic* understanding he should, in all earnestness (tapping my eyelid—pop pop pop), extricate his cornea.

You see, I snapped, my pink-you erect, *Anna and Helen drank tea in front of a fire and prepared the great cape of the matador as a gift for the daughter of God two (he) and God eighteen (she). God six (he), the death in man's eye god, and God seven (he), the minor philosophical texts god, recalled the life of God one (she). God one (she), the suffering of imaginary beings god, met her end by the doings of God three (she), the god of collective beneficence and God two (he), the god of tameable animals. God three (she) and God nine (she), dry places beneath a tree when it rains god, conceived but miscarried. God eighteen (she), god of unremembered faces, and God two (he), god of water poured from a vessel, were banished and had a child, God twenty-three (she), god of rare beauty.*

I concluded by unfurling my arms but he was crisp with me and punctuated his curiosity with the stunting of his wrist, though bouncy and slightly to the left. Moving about the train, I endeavoured to convince others of my dilemma Sad, sweet Helen, prisoner of God twenty-three (she). My melancholy made its way into her seams and curled beneath her dress into the shape of a spiral that once descended gave no hope of return. I thought if I were to play my loin for them, so sweetly and in such fine tune…the freight cars…the wheels…the smoke.

Oh! Le train!

Christmas last I related it thus: standing in the train station I waited for the b-l-a-n-k to Prague. A woman, whose name I wished [hello] to be Helen—yes? I found her arm and Anna strewn—nay, frolicking with the Gods. I remember remembering how they frolicked when a few days after I placed my advertisement in Le Monde, I received a phone call.

'Hello, I'm answering your advertisement,' the woman said.

'You have one arm?' I asked.

'Yes,' she said.

'And you are of a rare beauty?' I asked.

'I have tried,' she said. 'My mother was beautiful, but my father—'

'—and your name?' I asked. 'What is your name?'

Before she answered, I thought what if her name was Anna? Would that be okay? I remember remembering Anna. Poor disillusioned Anna whom I wished 'with all my heart'—no that was Helen. I thought no, her name had to be Helen.

'Your name,' I said impatiently.

'Elaine,' she said.

'Oh, that's lovely,' I said. 'I will you call you Elle. We must meet when I return.'

I remember remembering that I was eager but composed and that I ratified our future union with a pop of the wink-wink aluminium. After my stint in Prague, I would return a recaptured man. Oh the memory! It was all there. It came over me in a wave of something I had no idea about. I had so many questions for her. Which arm? How? I could hold her closer I thought. By my side, she would feel a part of me. And how my shoulder would tickle as I felt her nerve endings through her skin.

I stood proudly.

Dear passengers, I orated, *pick up your feet and run in happiness with me. I have lived many a life of experience and know this to be a good and measured response. Do not show* (I paused to find the right word) *conjecture. Run with me.*

I ran through the train, away from its destination and toward happiness, reflecting on the matador's lover who danced so intimately with another man that the pain the matador felt at seeing their intimacy was like the horn of the bull, stuck between his ribs and puncturing his heart. Oh, I felt it too. But if I were to dance with this beautiful woman, I would pull her very close to me and holding her from behind, probe the soft, sweet nape of her neck with my very sensitive nose.

I returned to my seat and rested my head against the window.

Are we not weary men Caesar?

I sighed. Such a long string to fiddle and me out of practice. Will it be Smetana or Dvořák? Now they were pretty girls with big lips and long eyelashes.

Not so weary that we cannot find our rest in chaos.

(colors, shapes, and everyness)

the unknowed things

the unknowed things

So sad to be alive. If it is a question of the interest
Archibald drums up it is good to sell. *Sad is a vitamin.*
She asked me: *what happened and where is the she?* I told her
I saw the car tire roll slowly over the boy's body and of
how I picked him up and of how he smiled at me
before I wept. Such [inaudible moaning] is the
precursor. In a cul-de-sac many years ago {name
unknowed} sat at a table and turned in his chair, lifting
his right arm and placing his right hand on his left wrist.
He looked to me. This was his milieu. I paused him
there and moved him from place to place. In the
elevator of my building, when the doors parted he
turned in his chair to see the arrival of many people. In
the forest outside the city, where I hid behind a tree, he
heard the wind and the water and the snapping of
branches.

It has been said that the first hand is the dilemma. What
to do with it? The second follows according to its
nature. The boy fell under the wheel. I moved hand one
but hand two did not follow. I pondered the nature of
this second hand as I hoped for the collapse of
something tangible in me. A collapse of the foundation
that kept this worthwhile (by all accounts) structure
upright and aware of its own milieu. But there was no
collapse even as I took apart what made it recognizable
to those who observed.

If a building is the cornerstone of 'civilization paths'
then Tangier deserves its place in geography. It was a
crummy way to start out on the golden trail but I had
asked nicely and was rewarded with a catheter to the
brain stem. Yesterday nothing drained but today was

frisky with no evidence of humanity in the atmosphere. The doctors said I drained an easily quantified amount of—and then a communal huddle followed by 'well, in any case, everything's fine'. I reassembled and set my oysters on history.

Everyone knows the plot thickens with the arrival of new invitees. I invited Perry. And then Lily. Likewise Jame. The last ounce of Jame dissolved in my preserves not long after her tale was {action unknown}. And don't forget the adventures of the cornbread maker who, despite his Marxist leaning, was always a hero to me. No one knew his real name, though I suspected it was one of those union monikers. The cornbread maker's second hand always followed accordingly.

We would hope that all futures have but one rule regardless of how those futures originate and that the wisdom of this one rule permeates false theories as well as true theories so the convergence of all that is true and false, although it does not provide the epiphany that would justify a mistaken life, at least makes one pause long enough to realize that the wisdom of this one rule is best and from here onward, there will be a new way.
--Vice Admiral Atsuko Miyazaki,
interviewed on the TV2 show 'It's in the Lips'

When the show ended, I wrote a letter in disagreement with the guest's views and harangued the ever-so 'quote, unquote' fair host for being a tool of the anti-{cause unknowed} propagandists. To my surprise, I received a response, stating that a vice admiral couldn't be blamed for the consequences of my ingratitude. Such a knowing people, I thought. It was true. Lily had given me everything even when I didn't ask, appearing with unexpected gifts even when I deserved nothing.

She told me the most beautiful stories that I, in turn, told to others as if they were my own.

She never said good-bye.

(Or maybe she did and I wasn't listening.)

In the dark end of the forest I see Frau Gretchen's pupae and then her milk situated just so beneath the ever impending palm of shuttle-shoots. We are of a like mind she and I. A minion crawling toward the calm underbrush of snow and the splintered trunk of Tiberius. She said all mornings remain the same. Just above the ground and into a thin forktwist that rebels against the natural movement of the promenade. Drill the {object unknowed} to ferment the dew, an approaching opening, something slender and orb, like the ascendance of a tyrant.

We stood there. Capable of movement but incapable of reason. In the parlance of 'what have we got here?' it was a preamble to a less derisive unknown: sadly, sniff sniff, on this day twenty years ago.

The portly frau misunderstood my discontent and compared it to the time she rolled her eyes at the largest animal enclosure on this side of the peninsula. Up on that hill, during winter, they found a pair of school-girl knickers covered in what could only be described as 'the perfume of the royal stem'.

Certainly, the populace had their druthers. But wiser men believed that such pungency came with a considerably more decisive incision, although it wasn't enough to sever the second hand—the worthless appendage that 1.) hung so proudly and 2.) sought only its advantage. The wives of these wiser men chanted as if in a trance: 'hack away at the bits and pieces of all it had done, all the vile, and all the sick'. And I confessed to an accomplice that it was a catchy little tune but the strength necessary for such a feat required two arms and the swing of a more foreign musculature.

Lily got down on all fours and asked me to soak in her sunshine. So warm and rubby on the face. A brilliant light that peeked through her whistle. It was a certain kind of paradise if only one could forget where one was.

But it wasn't enough to balm the infected blood, instead injecting more bile into the sting. And yet a bile that tasted like the most succulent honey the amazing honeybee had ever produced. Honey so angelic that it could only be crafted by the god of honey and honey bees. Honey that once coated the befuddled tongue of man made it a morsel that he nibbled on until he was mute and could only buzz-buzz-buzz the words he needed to say: *forgive me for all the wrong that I have done.*

It was a sickly episode. A black canard of an existence that served no purpose if one deed went undone. A puzzle that was none but chaos should one piece not be picked up and put in its proper place. A bird that would not fly should one feather be plucked and not reattached to its swollen dimple. There was time in all of this to make the right move. Frau Gretchen warned me. Jame. Spencer. They collaborated to collect my disjecta and set me on that golden trail. But Lily turned me away and had me roiling in so many timbers until the boy fell upon the ground and lay like peace in the universe.

On a warm night in Tangier, the carpenter falls in love.

I picked up his body and stood before a large window that drew my eyes to a garden where, in time, the existence of many secret villages were discovered: Sangiers and Fingiers, Longiers and Sungiers, pots and kettles, utensils for eating, hat making instruments and unused soles of shoes, moss covered dresses, pliers and balloons, shells of turtles, pictures of owls, indigenous kale, friends.

The boy smiled even as his eyes closed and I wondered why at this most important moment in human history, the sun did not part the clouds and light the most beautiful face that ever veiled the blood of man.

{end unknowed}

when boys sleep

when boys sleep

i?

When boys sleep, birds lift their wings to still the branches of trees.

There are events which take place before and after the end. Should a man enter the two spaces formed by these four boundaries he becomes lost for a while. Not very lost. But lost enough to think that he has taken this life for granted. He makes a promise to himself that before the next end, each minute he lives will burst from the amount of life he shall fill it with. He makes this promise secretly—while looking through the window of a bus or standing alone in the corner of an elevator.

He reasons at such moments that he is not very lost, after all, only a little. But in this reasoning germinates the tragedy of being only *a little lost*. He orbits the earth and seeing it *just over there* suffices.

ii?

When boys sleep, the majesty of their dreams are revealed in every drop of rain that falls, in every molecule of air that touches human face, in every cell that glides beneath human skin.

Today the mailbox is empty and I wait for a response. To think about the small room and just outside a forest of blueberries. The white desk. The photo albums and the diary with missing pages.

To think about the short walk to the river. Too long have I suppressed the memories of this life. Of the tree that fell and cleared a path through the clouds. A path to the future.

I make preparations. But in this room, the clouds are darkened by our shadows. Something happens here as Juliet blows the feather from her hand and I watch it float from the window onto the grass. With each turn in its descent, an old room in an old city and the horizon measured by old windmills, the sun three windmills wide and growing, the room five windmills slow as if a ship of long and faithful suffering.

We trace these movements to understand that our happiness is found in the smallest moments of doubt. In the nimble. In the crane on the horizon upon which a boy sits and spies us from the distance. In the faded and opened hand of a woman that can never be drawn again.

iii?

When boys sleep, the universe descends on mankind and for a short while the world trembles with meaning.

Metaphysics, it has been said, is an unwieldy feather and so we must sublimate the chaos of patterns created by the accidental motions of this feather in order to give us an image that approaches that thing for which there is no word.

But this feather is used in many ways. When Juliet moves it along my spine, I think about the room we are in and the window from where I see her bicycle leaning against the tree. When Juliet moves the feather along my spine, I think that I have lived in this room my whole life. With her. Between the soft, white blankets. In the melodies of Chopin. On the wooden floor. In the glass of water on the table through which I see man's caricature of time.

I feel her trace a question mark between my shoulders and we commit to each other's subtle rearrangements in silence. We know we are cursed, if only for a short while, to take our place among the living.

iv?

When boys sleep, the ruminations of future progeny fan our desires.

I sensed from the beginning Juliet's proclivity for distance. I met her by the fountain taking pictures and I moved towards her as if of some other will. In turn she moved and barely so to keep me at bay. I said to her from where I stood *there is a graceful way in which to view the gallows.*

Juliet and I eat at three feet. We sleep at two. We speak at five. So before she speaks she will move away from me. But not now, sitting here on the bed next to me, she draws a secret language on my skin that I will spend my day deciphering. Soon she will leave. Later she will return, leaning her bicycle against the tree, hurrying up the stairs to see me again, her body less of breath that she will encourage me to replace.

v?

When boys sleep, the truth veils itself so we cannot elude it.

The question mark is an ambiguous symbol. At one moment, a representation of deference. At another moment, of defiance. It provokes thought today and leaves the mind immobilized tomorrow. In all objects and gestures. In all faces and events. But at the end of all question marks, one will find a pause. A park bench on which to rest and watch pretty girls take pictures of bicycles and sailboats and of beautiful women talking quietly together by a fountain of horses in which their children play. In this place, such things are possible. The air is finer here. Our lungs more capable.

vi?

When boys sleep, the euphony of silence adorns our every word.

I knocked on the door and Juliet said *come in*. I sat down beside her on the bed and told her there is something I feel that I cannot put into words. Something about lions and long strands of hair. A pillow and a breeze. She said she felt it too. I took her hand and held it without speaking.

Behind us, the window framed the image of a crane on the horizon, upon which a boy and his sleep created all that was dreamed and not dreamed in this small patch of world that was ours.

vii?

When boys sleep, that which is immutable fragments and finds shelter in the dreams of children.

All one need do is peek through the window. On the crane in the distance, the boy sleeps in the dimly lit night. His face, an image of peace and love. In cities all over the world, known and unknown to you, when the sun sets and his eyes start to close.

In Rotterdam. In Dublin. In Glasgow. In *Trondheim.* In Bucharest. In *Borås.* In Helsinki. In St. Petersburg. In Shanghai. In Kyoto. In Lille. In Darfur. In Asmara. In Kuala Lumpur. In Ulan Bator. In Perth. In Bombay. In Lima. In Des Moines. In Alberta. In Juneau. In *Skeldon.* In Machico. In Barcelona. In Sarajevo. In *Washington D.C.*

viii?

When boys sleep, all that is beautiful in this world ascends.

Juliet and I ride our bicycle between the rows of mist. Above, a boy the shape of life and what it is to be living curls up and wrenches our plot asunder. A bobwit and allegory of pending trifles, he senses to me her ankle and supple calf, a whittle of such splendor as to make a weighty man no more than an ounce. But there is a strong gust from the horizon and we pound the grind racing, drifting onward into that orbit spoke of but never again, circling the trolley and the carriage and the flat boat on the canal, leaning from the bridge to drink where children play without surrender, a pardon, a sense of grace, turning and turning and turning.

ix?

When boys sleep, all that we have seen and heard and learned is returned to the place of its birth.

Bring out the trotters and me a captive in this room. Their bright regalia and nostrils of flame but fearful of those children who adore them. She (9 hers) pulls love from my mouth and cups it in her hands. We build a tree there and a sailboat of wood, a bicycle for two, a dock from which to leap, and with the flip of a switch, a bright and promising sun. We are afraid to move. While we are here. Closer and closer and closer we stand and in so doing, darken the clouds.

(viremia)

(viremia)

Beauty brings an end to all hope and as such perpetrates a *decelerative force* on existence. To say it differently, as we are inclined to do, if only for the reason that we can: our hopes end in beauty.

To term this force in such a manner is to give the reader a positive impression of beauty and to defend beauty from its truth.

Some say that beauty needs defending and that its truth lies not in its negative nature but elsewhere. To these people we say poppycoodle. As drumming is a prima facie form of gesticulation, the former being in and of itself the latter (note the paradox), the whole kitten caboodle of beauty relinquishes itself in its ultimate realization and reveals the cynical nature of its drive.

If we turn one eye to the Renaissance with its illusory hubbub, we might see a harlequin dancing, a juggler of bread, a pope-stroking official of letters but {burble} here sits a wooden brawl with one mango and papaya, just as it sat so many centuries ago. It is no surprise then that the Renaissance can be considered the first phase of that oft over-used articulation known as *movement*. And this *movement* is at once the beginning and the end of itself, for there can be no end without burble [hyphen] burble.

Lament, denial, destiny...

Despite the metaphysical throat clearing of philosophers, one stumbles upon the gist of what these philosophers cough up. This gist itself is not important.

What is important is that this gist is not sufficient to fill the tum tum of the little birdy it is intended to feed. Nor is it for that matter (cough) representative of a value-inducing praxis.

So, what to make of all manner of hindrance that approximates this decelerative force without actually becoming it?

For the answer, we turn our other eye to Gogol and his 'festive pontoon' [i.e. orion's nutmeg]. Gogol's 'festive pontoon', though seemingly explicit and denotative, once deconstructed invites further plumbing.

Hurtigruen gurty flimson…the…fa…la…twinkle

Stripped of its literary veneer, Gogol's 'festive pontoon' reveals a striking parallax. Astonishingly, hope, with its characteristic p, u, pute, and c is the poison that brings the patient to our attention.

Oh hope. Oh transcendent, mortifying castaway of our solipsy. Were it not a fright to be such plumbed, a good hearty plumbing t'would bon vivant licky.

With these words, justly or unjustly, Gogol destroyed the language of the bourgeoisie, and in so doing destroyed the settee of beauty's lap dog. It becomes apparent, as appearance is the end all and be all of being, that beauty is the succorer of all evil in this world. For what is the death of hope if not evilness. And yet, hope itself is evilness.

Vile. Venal. Vindictive. Vengeful. Venomous.

Beauty, undressed once and for all, cowered at the sight of Gogol's sword and vanished with the language that spawned it.

Oh, only if it were so…

So what of this supposed destruction? Why is the language of the bourgeoisie still babbled today long after Gogol's resounding victory? The answer is as simple as it is cozy. The bourgeoisie's methods of retaliation are brutal and irrevocable (note the awful manner in which the Italians are treated) and include co-option and disregard. With co-option, victory for the likes of Gogol is unattainable.

'Bon vivant licky licky', mobli.

'hamaji corn plutefar?'

For Gogol, who stripped beauty down to its asshole, disregard for the destruction he inflicted restored beauty and hope as the center pieces of the holy-shit-not-that-shit-again-claptrap-hey-I-wanna-hear-it-all-again-in-the-only-way-I-know-how bullshit.

{Ethiopian, Etruscan, and Coptic wheat snack}.

This gestural dismissal of the destruction is evidence that the importance of the 'festive pontoon' is not found in its answer to the age-old question, but in the way this answer reinvents the question.

Beauty, a hobknob, gestural in its connotation, soothier, darker, and more insinuating.

However, despite the bourgeoisie's seemingly effective disregard, what we find in 'the festive pontoon' is the victory of a single mind over all of mankind. Unnoticed, sad, a little plump, and possibly squirmy.

the history of imagining about blue horses

the history of imagining about blue horses

the blue horse

Sebastian San Miguel sat on the bench in the small park across the road from Santa Maria and watched its large wooden doors through the branches of the flowering trees. He hoped the cathedral noticed he was dressed in his nicest suit and best hat and that he sat patiently and gently on the bench without so much as a gesture that might be mistaken for insistence. He thought let it be known from the tipping of my hat and the crossing of my legs that I shall sit and enjoy this day and expect nothing; that I shall treat my time upon this bench frivolously and read my book and be distracted by passing clouds. He thought this sincerely although he hoped the large wooden doors of Santa Maria would open and the sound of the organ would move down the concrete steps leading to the road and without pausing for traffic, cross over and sit down beside him like someone he didn't know. Like someone who might say hello and smile then open a book to start reading only to close it again and sit quietly for a few moments before turning to him to address the strange blueness of the sky.

i paused and the world swallowed me

Martin closed his book and drank his coffee. Alice was still sleeping so he made up his mind to take a walk through the city. He looked through the open window from the small kitchen and saw the cathedral above the trees. He inhaled the newness of another day and all that it brought with it. He wanted to tell Alice what he thought about the blue horse in the book he was reading but he was afraid that the telling of the thought would ruin the thought itself. He believed one must step delicately upon such matters. He could tell Alice because she usually gave a brief but thoughtful reply and that was all he wanted. He wasn't interested in the indifferent chit-chat of someone who didn't care or the lengthy conversation of the well-read on such matters. For these were matters, he believed, that were of such importance that they should be treated with reverence, understanding, and most of all, brevity.

He rinsed his cup and placed it in the sink. He picked up his book and grabbed his jacket from the hook by the front door. The caption above his head as he paused in the open doorway read *filled with possibilities.*

the alice mystery

Alice puts on the robe resting on the chair by the vanity. She pulls her hair back into a ponytail and clasps it with a hair band. She walks into the living room and picks up a magazine about the architecture of Barcelona. Alice feels she has something important to do today. She's not sure what it is but she knows she will do it.

In the kitchen she sees a cup in the sink and rinses it before pouring some coffee that Martin has already made. She stands by the window and sees the cathedral above the trees. She wonders if Martin will return before she must go out and do the thing. The thing. She puts the cup down and returns to the bedroom. She lies down, looks out into the living room, and twirls the edges of her pillow.

the letter n is an alphabet

The blue horse was unmistakable but what to make of the old man on the bench Martin thought? He had ideas. Ideas that turned in his head while he walked until they coalesced into one single thought. But should he utter the thought? Would it survive? It was not a reflection on the strength or beauty of the thought if once it passed his lips, it lost its wonder and shrivelled up and died. It was simply a difference of atmosphere. Perhaps he would hide the thought by wrapping many words around it. Hide it from those who would damage it. And those who were predestined for it would see it there in the middle, protected by letters and words and pauses that were of little consequence to the thought itself. He had done this sort of thing with Alice. Not about books or ideas but about her. Thoughts about Alice had often come to him that were so beautiful, so magical, so fragile, that death was a certainty for them if they were spoken. So he brought them into this world hidden in long sentences that often had Alice shaking her head.

'What are you saying?' she would say. 'Why can't you just say what you are saying?'

'It's like with the books,' Martin would say. 'You know.'

And then the phone would ring or a song would play and a few minutes later the thought was forgotten.

the architecture of Barcelona

There is more to Barcelona than Gaudi. There are the huts of the hill people made out of human hair and the skeleton of animals. There are the rhubarb shaped houses made out of sea-salt and wood flown in from Zaire that pock the city's perimeter. There are several apartment buildings, the foundations of which are constructed of a rare fungus that can only be found in northern Spain. There is the train station, a creation of oversized children's blocks with reinforced glass holding them all together. There is the Museum of Literature, the only one of its kind anywhere in the world except Dusseldorf, an amalgam of telephone metal and camel glue. And then there is Carmen and so on and so forth...

the bounty of my wry divisions

What was Alice up to Sebastian San Miguel wondered? He had an inclination to turn to the pages at the end of the book to find out. There was always that danger with him for he had become impatient as he grew older.

He glanced over to the cathedral doors but they were still closed. The organ must play today he thought. Today of all days. Of all days, today. Perhaps Santa Maria had noticed. Perhaps Sebastian San Miguel had revealed his desire in the hasty way he turned the pages of his book. Or perhaps he had shaken his leg without realizing it. If he could manage to distract himself for a few minutes—to think about everything but the organ—there might still be a chance that the doors of the great cathedral would open.

what alice didn't do

Alice didn't go to the market today or stop for chocolate and pastries at her favorite café. She didn't paint the bathroom wall orange or model nude. She didn't exchange her pesos for crowns or feed pigeons along the rue. She didn't walk by the river and wish it were warmer. She didn't wash the dishes. She didn't have this conversation.

'Tendrils fire uncertain three times from my boon', she didn't say.

'Insolent let me spench, then free', he didn't respond.

'If only it were so', she didn't say.

'Are we speaking of more than what is here?' he didn't ask.

'Don't be stupid', she didn't say.

Then she didn't turn away.

the boy

A friend who I hadn't seen in years stood in front of me. I asked him what he was doing here and he said his father had moved to Barcelona because he learned how to draw. He said he was there to take me to my boy. I would like that very much I said. Very much. Nine long months have I been pregnant for him. So we drove to the street near Santa Maria and parked.

I can only tell you what I saw that day as I waited in the car. Two men were sitting on a bench in the park. A young man closed a book he was reading and turned to an old man. Then the large, wooden doors of Santa Maria opened and a blue horse with a woman riding upon it walked slowly out and made its way down the steps. It stood there, this blue horse with the woman sitting on its back, its large eyes reflecting the skyline of Barcelona and the apartment window where the face of another woman slowly descended like the sun on a faraway horizon.

chalker

chalker

Our garden rain petunias have died but we waited until morning to notice.

We lay on the hill and counted the airplanes go by until night covered our bodies like a silk blanket and buried us in the grass. You said it was impossible to imagine the sky with three suns. Not impossible I said, but it would only be thrilling if imagined. Imagine, I said, if they were really there. Then it would be thrilling to imagine the sky with only one, you said.

Remember the day the constable knocked on our door and asked us if we had heard any noises outside? We had heard nothing but I was in my pajamas and you were upstairs taking a bath. That was the day rabbits played by the window.

Or maybe the grass was a bed that night lay upon and so light as to not disturb us it slept and perhaps dreamed of us and all that had happened to it as day.

You called airplanes 'chalker'. And I couldn't disagree with you or tell you otherwise because I saw the lessons too. Saw the letters and numbers and angles they drew to explain the strange flowers that grew from mama's head. But we never remembered the lessons. Better to forget them you said and continue to see things with wonder.

'You are my sword', I'd say.

To others it may have seemed that you ignored me, but I knew better because you'd ask me to tell you what I was thinking.

'What?' I'd ask. 'What am I thinking?'

'You know', you'd say.

'I don't know', I'd say.

'Oh come on say it', you'd say.

'You mean what I say all the time?' I'd say.

'Yes, come on, just say it and get it over with', you'd say. 'You know.'

'I love you', I'd say.

And then you'd laugh and I'd shake my head and laugh a little bit too.

You said it's no fun to imagine just one sun when you've already imagined three. You're right, I said. Tomorrow three suns will rise in such a way that there will be no night. No, you said. Let them rise all at once and set all at once and that would allow things to be dreamed of. In the morning we'll tie a rope from one tree to the other and slide across it. Maybe the grass will sweep our feet clean so mama won't have to follow us around with the broom.

But that night as we lay upon the grass and forgot lessons we learned earlier in the day, we saw what night dreamed. A carousel of space between spinning horses.

A cape and you in shoes too big. Us drenched in rain and laughing. And we looked at each other and smiled because it was what we wanted. It was what we always wanted.

Mama opened the window to look at us and cried and you asked me why. Because she knows that one day we'll hear the noises outside, I said. But not yet. Tomorrow three suns will rise and it will be more beautiful than we ever imagined.

theophilus god

theophilus god

When Trevor investigated the bureaucracy, he uncovered ample evidence of someone tampering with its machinery: a violin bow leaning carefully beneath the on/off switch and a puddle of urine seeping near the generator fan.

'Don't step in it,' he told passersby. 'It's evidence.'

Prague had become a desert. All the buildings were gone. That one man, and a violinist at that, could destroy a great city, was unfathomable to Trevor. His main suspect, Theophilus God, the self-proclaimed *conducteur de composeur* passed his fate of an unfulfilled destiny (of an early death) onto his boy. *Go well* he whispered into his boy's cold ear all the while thinking about fingering Maria, who expressed her sympathies to him with tears and the *odeur* of a rather provocative *eau de toilette*.

How to get in there he wondered as his upper lip felt the chill of his son's bloodless cheek. He pulled back slowly and wiped his mouth.

'Yucky death,' he whispered to himself. 'Yucky.'

He thought there would be no speeches for his boy. Let him go unencumbered by false accounts that he would only be burdened with setting right in some other place.

'Sorry for your loss,' Hesmodina God said. His cousin. 'We crossed the Atlantic to be here.'

And it was as if the word 'atlantic' became a key that slipped into his notch, and turning him sideways, placed him next to his boy where he wept like he had never wept before. He heard the ocean in his head, saw the hard water, the vastness of it, and a blissful oblivion overcame him from where he thought no return was possible. Death must be like something he thought. Like a brick. Like a stone. And he conceded that one day some little bastard would kick him along the grass. Theophilus God resting beneath a tree, brainless, and with no other purpose than to be kicked. He couldn't even say he was resting. He would just be there.

Trevor didn't care. He'd show up at the funeral with cars and badges and sniffing dogs.

Maria stroked Theophilus God's hair but he was no longer interested in fingering her. That such a thought could enter his mind at such an occasion seemed grotesque to him now. Finger Maria? Finger her? What did it mean?

'Theophilus God,' she said. 'There are mutants in our life when we can only be weak.'

'Mutants?' Theophilus God asked.

'You know what I mean,' Maria said and showed him this picture she had drawn on the back of a napkin (mankind's second greatest invention):

Theophilus God dropped to his knees and while thanking Maria for her understanding, realized this was as close as he would ever get to fingering her. He could put his arms around her and his nose would be right there. He heard his tongue moving inside his mouth. He hated himself for the thought but it was okay to hate himself because he only wanted to die. *Oh death, come for me.* But it didn't come and a few minutes later, back on his feet with pure thoughts, he was thankful.

'Maria,' he said. 'You have always been a friend to me.'

Maria agreed.

As the self-proclaimed *conducteur de composeur*, Theophilus God believed that an infinite symphony had already composed itself and that his existence represented only two notes in that symphony. But they were two notes the symphony could not be without.

Just *ping* and then *pung* and his life would be over. His boy was *pang* and *da da da* and he supposed that if his boy had *pang*ed *or da da da*-ed one more time the symphony would stop in a crash of cymbals and the world would end nigh.

Trevor walked in on the occasion and made himself noticed with the clacking of his cane against the jamb. Oh, it was no accident. It was a sturdy cane but not heavy and Trevor wielded it adeptly. Theophilus God heard the clack and recognized the key shift to minor that Trevor brought with him.

He had written a letter to Trevor once, imploring him to investigate the haughtiness of certain neighbors who felt compelled to castigate him for his musical endeavors. The letter was a mistake however, for Trevor's suspicious appetite soon found sustenance on Theophilus God himself. Questions were asked, questionnaires were delivered, messages were sent.

The neighbors answered unanimously: *Theophilus God was a man of dangerous quantities.*

In fact, just the other night he saw music from an unplayed measure and had not completely recovered. Oh, the monstrosity of infinite knowledge, he thought. To see but one note from the future was too strenuous for the human mind. And yet the pull of it. It tugged at him in his dreams, in slips of the tongue, in barely conscious thoughts so delicate that a whispered word put to them would immediately be their destruction. He got down on his knees again and thought about fingering Maria.

Yes, finger her. Finger her until she moaned like a prophet.

Such thoughts were indestructible. Such thoughts blunted even the finest poetry.

Trevor put his hand on Theophilus God's shoulder and showed him the violin bow he found by the generator fan. Behind Trevor, Theophilus God saw Hesmodina God brushing her daughter's fine, golden hair. The girl waved to him and he thought about snapping twigs with her beneath a tree and throwing them at the tree's big, uneven trunk.

'Theophilus,' she'll say, 'I like you.'

And he'll pick up a stone and put it in her pocket.

'Keep it safe,' he'll tell her.

And then he'll wait beneath the tree, until she is older to share her first heartbreak with her.

Maria intervened.

'How can you do this now?' she asked and walked away.

Do what now Maria?

Trevor took him by the arm and led him through the doors, out into that once great city that was now a wasteland of brick and stone. Theophilus God chuckled.

'What?' Trevor asked.

'You'll never—,' Theophilus God fell to the ground.

'I'll never what?' Trevor giggled.

'You'll never find the violin,' Theophilus God said and he laughed until he peed his pants.

the purpose of green in the bikini machine
shop

the purpose of green
in the bikini machine shop

The bikinis passed overhead on hangers, dripping their green dye onto the floor, tapping undecipherable code as I considered the events of the previous day. I remembered Gregor Samsa and how he couldn't stop dropping things as he crawled from exit to exit inspecting the amount of light coming into the factory.

The first of the week was always the most difficult and unaccommodating as pressers relaxed in anticipation of the coming days. It took a heavy toll on us and I fear that it will last until the day we die. Minutes are stolen quietly in such places and dropped into someone else's clock before we realize what has happened. But I know because I have deciphered the code.

The first tap of the drip green is a lie but I am not fooled. *Fair bright fading kiss.* Kill and kill and kill. I'm riding my bicycle (bicycle) home.

It was simpler when it was only once upon a time, before the nimble life or a beheading to order cracked like a nut from paradise to inferno with just this lay bare in between. This.

Fucking thing. I twirl between two fingers and roll into the palm of my hand.

But what of the noise? And the grinding? And the textured electricity that hides rage behind something called—I don't want to say…

Gregor Samsa said let us be numb and give language only shells to batter. Not cannonade or abuse or hit or stamp or pummel...

Legs walk and compass remote from my expectation. There were high windows all round and the way someone stood with their head down told us nothing. And I knew it was always like this—that silence told us nothing even though we were led to believe otherwise and think of our paltry moments as gifts holding mystery.

Once upon a time:

A boy received a hat for his birthday, wore it to school and made lights change along the way, made other kids spell hard words, made them run faster when they played.

Once upon a time:

All I ever wanted was everything and to live between the tops of trees.

tap...tap...tap...tap...

Green is the color of my genie. I'll say it (swinging) again because (unthunder) it doesn't seem (slow motion rhino) to be getting through.

But there is work to do in the bikini machine shop and the bikinis pass overhead on hangers, dripping their green dye onto the floor. I hear the whistle-not-proper connect me to ear-transparent's wunderkind though not enough to hide the tapping uncoded second pause. A movement glib with skin and blood and the stretching of their connection. Pulled from the bone and nibbled on by impending.

It's been wonderful.

But where is the girl? She is there. Sitting two rows over by the wall. Black hair down to her shoulders, covering most of her face but not enough to stop me from wanting to reach across space to touch her.

That small piece of skin is enough for now.

And then the bell rings and the bell rang and the bell will ring and the bell would have rung and the bell should have rung and the bell could have rung and the bell is ringing.

Once upon a time.

the last of the undressed children has run by

the last of the undressed
children has run by

a dark place of sadness and heartbreak

In Demerara palm trees exist. Clothiers tailor umbrellas. The hat brim of an old man looking down at his shoes gives one a feeling of inevitability. What once was, no longer is, and the drawings of giraffes and owls on the shower glass are washed away. Out there in the city the news girl stands in the middle of the road by a streetlight, fanning herself with the morning edition, shouting *young boy drowns in the river.*

Martin didn't want such things to be true but he knew they were true because life was like that. Things that shouldn't happen happen and if it weren't for a certain hardness in him, he believed he would collapse and die from pity. For he believed that pity—real pity—brought on a terminal condition. A dark place of sadness and heartbreak he was always trying to find a way out of.

three and 1/fertile

The old man took off his hat and placed it near the crumpled newspaper on the space beside him. He pulled back his long, stringy hair and rubbed both eyebrows with the tips of his fingers. He had come a long way from what he always wanted. Now he wanted to be an army ranger and shoot people. Maybe save a little girl from being raped by guerillas and carry her to the safety of a helicopter. Old men had dreams too.

He pulled off his shoe and turned it upside down so that a small pebble fell out. He leaned down to look at it and his head dropped to the floor and rolled for three and a half miles before it stopped against the post of a broken-down, wooden fence that separated the road from the jungle.

tar-mata

When the news girl walked into the small open space of the shop, the city came with her. The tops of buildings. Trees. The corrugated balconies and the clothes that hung over them. The glistening of traffic. The telephone wires. The noise. The clouds. The sun. They followed her wherever she went because they liked her. But the news girl wasn't particularly fond of them. She could do without the tops of buildings and the noise on most days. And she didn't have much use for balconies or the clothes hanging over them. The trees served her well on certain days when she didn't care much for the sun and the sun served her well on days when the clouds darkened her mood. She didn't think much about telephone wires. And the glistening of traffic bothered her eyes.

'What's for lunch?' she asked.

Sasha, who had been rubbing an apron against a wooden washboard, wiped the sweat from her forehead, and said: 'drumsticks'.

Martin sat at one of the tables near the window. Outside it became dark. He felt the marrow in his femur and heard a clicking sound that reminded him of pellet.

marrow

We all have marrow in our femur. It's not a plight and perhaps even conducive to a certain way of living. Tent-like. Or house-like. Possibly vine-like. Sometimes Tunta, despondent over his lack of tribute, played like he didn't get it. It wasn't believable, of course, because everybody gets it. Sometimes they go. Dress willy, for example. Or salt. And then there's the whole story of the shop sign. About how in future history books (or dictionaries), the word 'rose' will come to mean 'slab' or 'dark terror of stone'. But let us save that for the future.

For now: to every traveler, a place to rest.

ingomar

When Robert found the head near the post of the wooden fence that separated the jungle from the road, the mouth on the head had a smile on it, which made Robert think that the person who belonged to the head, smiled when the end came. But this wasn't true. You see, all that rolling along the road, hitting rocks and twigs and just your usual defects on a road that goes from city to country warped the old man's head so that it looked like there was a smile on his face when it finally came to a stop. But no, he wasn't smiling when the end came.

what once was, no longer is

There are explanations for most—what shall we call them?—occurrences. But *what once was, no longer is* requires a more erudite explanation than usual. It was a foreshadower.

Martin wanted to take the taxi with the news girl to the river. Not with Sasha. Sasha worked at the shop. The news girl's leg is what Martin turned around to look at before he walked into the shop. The news girl and her leg came in later. Sasha, on the other hand, didn't show her leg. She did, however, show the back of her head, most of her forehead and part of her face. Martin didn't see any of Sasha so he sat down at a table and looked through the window. It was then that he saw the news girl walking towards the shop and children running across the road behind her. It was only when the news girl came into the shop that Martin noticed Sasha. But Martin got up and moved to the balcony so that when the news girl left, he and the balcony left with her.

sondrine

Everyone knows the headlines. But are people aware of what's buried in the newspaper? The old man understood the print. The texture. But most of all he understood that it was the crinkly sound and the tiny little holes of the paper that revealed the details.

Most headlines were uninteresting: *D'Artagnan retired, Eliza Farthingbottom wrangled cattle in stilettos.*

But the old man listened to his newspaper. First he spied the holes to see how it should be played and then he slowly began to turn sections of the newspaper in his hand until he had gotten every last crinkly sound out of it. He could tell you things that the words were trying to conceal. How a 'u' might swallow the 'o' above it. Or how an 's' might uncoil itself and disappear into the grass.

glass

Martin looked through the window. He saw the news girl standing in the middle of the road. With his index finger he traced the outline of her body on the glass. He traced the traffic light beside her. Above her head he drew a small circle for the sun.

how things are hidden

The boy came from behind a palm tree near the river. He dashed over to the fence, naked and dripping wet, and picked up the head that lay near the fence post. He took the head with him and jumped back into the water and swam to the bottom of the river before making his way past the drawings of owls, past the news girl shouting, past Martin on the balcony, past the chalker, past the rose, past the fence, past the umbrella, past Sasha and the washboard, past the sun and the noise and the glistening of traffic until he found the old man sitting on the bench. He swam over to him and placed his head back onto his body. And then he took the hat from the chair and placed it on his head.

The old man's eyes opened for a moment and he looked around before he went back to sleep. On the brim of his hat written in small letters was the word *finito*.

beth v. beth singular

beth v. beth singular

Beth Susan has hyper-extended lymph nodes.

In the evenings she cooks or bakes. Never both. Sometimes she glazes a turkey before she puts it in the oven. There's no need to tell the story of her life because it can be summed up in this way: she is an ordinary person of ordinary ability. If one were to search for any magic in her routine, one would curse her existence. We could say she had choices. Instead of going here she might have gone there. Instead of doing this she might have done that. But if we curse her let us remember that she is not entirely to blame. At a young age she was set on a certain path and she continued along that path knowing nothing more.

And yet let us suppose she did know more. Let us suppose that at the age of twelve she saw a picture of Mongolian horses and later that night dreamed of palm trees. Perhaps—but really, what good would it have done? The courage to take a false step was not in her.

We'll say remember but it's not always about memory. The first virgin of civilization swept the streets outside her hut. There were the Francophiles and the Anglophiles but none restored order to the universe. So memory doesn't always hold sway. Doesn't reach out. Doesn't get Beth Susan wet. The most we can do for her is to glorify the ordinary. To say, for example, that the sun reaches her kitchen floor from a window through which she sees the grass and the overhanging branches of a nearby tree.

In time she became a precedent. A figure of imaginable awe. And then a subterranean falter of paprika and marmalade as she brought the curtain to the porch and spread it on the floor, searching for the circles and swelled-Friday in a singular expression of darker turning. Sensitive (sensitive) girl.

I knocked at a noble hour and upon being invited in said: 'Good morning Beth Susan'.

The day before, on a Sunday, pommes frijoles were served by the carpenter who designated the house and specifically the bedroom, the bed, and Beth Susan as things and person to think of while shuddering.

'Good morning', she said.

I sat for a coffee and remarked casually as to the paint peeling on the outside of her door. A sad summary for such a golden block or not quite, but close. She stared.

It is remarkable Beth Susan, your lumps are figuratively to die for and may I without regret continue my sympathy and curiosity for the sake of conversation. Laud me but make no mention of what is base as some poet might say for the sake (again) of sounding profound. But I have dreamed of you as if on a boat on a still, black sea. And the night. And the stars. How to make mention of them as they are? But may I, as I have always wanted, be the first to say that your sorrow is mine. It is mine and I come to take it from you.

Languid night. Three pence fold (comes the stolid).

The mollification of her stamina, free but not without its proclivities, proved a disaster to the carpenter, who hammered immorally throughout the house. Lest she forget the importance of shingles and their proper nailing I casually suggested an inspection of their aft and foreaft.

'Have you felt a…what shall I call it? A transition in your ear?'

She responded to the contrary but did confess, albeit reluctantly, of a colorless blur. The garments, the placards, the restive clink. I sensed her desire to keep them hidden. But what of the curtain Beth Susan? Is it not a child of the tropics? Relate this to me and in such a way as to approve of blood.

The Mongolian horses etc., etc. The palm trees, etc., etc.

So she's not the girl sitting on the couch. Her walls aren't blue. She doesn't have a ponytail or wear old shoes that have become fashionable.

Beth Susan, let me take your sorrow. It belongs to me. We are but two creatures you and I, an irrelevant species, hard pressed to die without a feeling of relief. The last feeling. The truest feeling.

drowning maria

drowning maria

When Maria looked out through the tall, open window at the single palm tree on the beach and how the large, flat leaves swayed to the measure of her tapping fingers, she thought back to a time when leaves weren't so friendly to her, when they chased her through the streets of her childhood neighborhood, scraping the concrete violently behind her. Now she was the master of them and tapped her fingers quietly to lull them into sway without alarming them. As a child she longed for winter and snow when the trees were bare and the ground covered so that she might explore the world without anxiety. But in this place she thought it impossible that winter could ever exist again. She would reach out to some distant feeling of ringing bells and the smell of oranges and burning wood but she could never get a hold of it.

In a few weeks she'll return to Chile for her friend's wedding. In a few months she'll ride her bicycle to the apartment of Gaston Ribera for a surprise visit and find him having breakfast with a woman she doesn't know. In a few years, she'll drink coffee at Mere Juni at the same time every evening and fall in love with the young painter who waits tables and who will change the landscape of art with Piñeroism—a play on his name and the word pin—that will be the start of her unhappiness.

But this morning she tapped her fingers quietly and prefaced the day with a hushed but candid confession to the palm tree about the orgasm she had the night before as she masturbated to the vicar's memory. It was the young vicar's fault she thought for being born so handsome but having become so unattainable. In turn, the night gave birth to a day that felt limitless and opened to her every whim.

She felt as she sat there listening to the ocean that she loved the world again, loved everything and everyone in it, loved humanity with all of its grand and not so grand gestures and foibles, loved the impudence of life in the seemingly endless void that was the universe. And yet, she felt unable to express her feeling in any understandable way.

Go well in this world and may no harm come to you. Be happy. Love. Laugh. Live.

She often thought these things to herself but could never say them to anyone. So she left friends and strangers alike with a smile they might think out of place or an awkward gesture or phrase they shook their heads to once out of her view. What to make of her they thought? What to make of what she said? What to make of the strangely awkward but graceful way she spoke with her hands? Perhaps they thought her naïve, but they'd forget this part of her soon enough as they went on to do things—important things, vital things, serious things, things that mattered—and this part of her would drift anonymously in and out of their lives. Or perhaps they pretended not to recognize this part of her and instead addressed her as if this part of her didn't exist because this part of her always felt out of context to them.

'How are you? Good good. Things are moving. Things are happening. Things. Yes yes. Things I tell you. Things. Moving moving moving. Things are moving.'

I met her those few weeks later at her friend's wedding. She sat alone in the church and stared at the fresco on the ceiling. Outside, I spoke to her and asked her if she knew the history of the fresco. She said she didn't so I told her the story of how the great Spanish artist Mirona was commissioned by the governor of the colony to paint memories of home and images of Heaven onto the ceiling of the church. Mirona painted for seven years and when he finished, he unveiled for the governor and colony officials a painting of poverty and suffering, of starvation and cruelty, of torture and deprivation with smiling angels and cherubs interspersed throughout. The governor ordered Mirona to repaint the ceiling or be put to death. Mirona refused. Another artist covered Mirona's fresco with plaster and painted a fresco more to the governor's liking. But there below the surface of this painting, the other painting still exists.

She seemed genuinely interested and questioned me as to the truthfulness of this tale. I assured her that although she wouldn't find this story in any book that it was entirely true. One need only chip away at those shining images of God and paradise on the ceiling above.

Perhaps when she rode her bicycle to visit Gaston Ribera, she thought back on this story and remembered my face. Remembered how we spoke briefly after a wedding outside an old church and then said goodbye. Maybe when she found Gaston Ribera in his apartment having breakfast with another woman she thought that she could have been with me instead, lying in bed, thinking about how it might be possible to unpaint a fresco in an old Spanish church. But we had said goodbye a long time ago and now she was riding away from his apartment in tears.

But why move ahead? Why let this blissful moment of her watching a single palm tree on the beach sink into the cloudy pool of memory? It would all end soon enough. One day her portrait, painted in the Piñeroistic style, will hang from that very wall behind where she is sitting and watch as she walks into the ocean and disappears.

observations on a future death

observations on a future death

6. nights like me }

I am of several minds and can't be with you today. Over here they're talking about war and pushing drunks in wheelbarrows to the safety of barges. Dogs smell tungsten and whimper in the unofficial language of despair. Nights like this make men famous. But not for long.

On the rubble of my old balcony Ludmilla cuts my hair. She talks and I listen.

'After this is over I'm going to open a salon', she says.

I mutter 'mhm' and that's her cue to continue. I hear the snips of the scissors in my head and her words start to disappear.

Ludmilla and I have no obligations tomorrow or the day after tomorrow. We're free from the life we hate. Free from time. But this freedom is sinister. This freedom has teeth and eats the weak. Ludmilla and I are weak. I think we will be dead by morning. I don't tell her that I think this. I let her cut my hair. I let her talk about after.

4. of this world +

Several minds make up a man. Several drives. This is the characteristic of the soul. This thing. The soul. That no one can describe. This is the soul.

I look at my hands and think that I have nothing. Nothing but this language I can't silence anymore. This language that tells me I have nothing. That I've always had nothing. This language that comes to me as an allergic reaction to everything I see or hear. It's there and it's grinding.

I feel like grabbing Ludmilla by the throat but I suddenly hear her talking again. I hear the snipping of the scissors. I think that Ludmilla is a child and I want to protect her. But this language triggers chemicals that in turn trigger this body. And if this body does nothing, it will die.

2. the great knee of shaka zulu ^

When Shaka Zulu fell on his knee he cried out in pain. Later it was written that he said 'There is nothing more powerful than the knee of Shaka. Nothing more beautiful. Nothing more perfect.' And for a long time throughout the tribal lands and all the British and French colonies one often said something along the lines of 'last night the sunset was as beautiful as Shaka's knee' or 'Ludmilla danced as gracefully as Shaka's knee'. The knee of Shaka Zulu was the end of all things. The end of all perfection. One might have even whispered in the corners of some church in England that 'the Lord is as powerful as the knee of Shaka Zulu'. But one never whispered 'more powerful'.

9. saturday afternoon carcass burn &

There is a fire in the land of the Cypriots. A gas tank celebration fitting for the times. If a thing should burn, whether it be thing or thing, then stand aside and let it burn. This is the proper attitude of the powerless who find something approaching their dreams in a good, hot fire that disintegrates the land. The Cypriots indulge in small things. Small things are the loose thread of the pallbearer's shoe. The pallbearer's shoe is a well-travelled instrument of the foot.

1. up here behind for the sun =

Some decline occurs so quietly over a long period of time that one will feel powerless to reverse it once it is noticed. One day some enticing stranger will ask: did you see that? And you will raise an eyebrow and while saying 'no', think to yourself *why didn't I see it? What has happened? It's been there all the time hasn't it? I thought the world had changed. When did it start?*

But it started when you started. You think it will take a long time to turn it back. And this stranger, though enticing, will not help you. You will wonder why. But there is a joy in this stranger's apathy you have lost and may never find again.

5. upheaval <

Mother and child left in the middle of the night. Mother packed their belongings into one box and drove away from Sarajevo. Ludmilla was only a baby and she cried all the way. I think Ludmilla sensed upheaval. I think upheaval stayed with her all her life and that she searched for a place where upheaval didn't exist. But the simplest things complicate a life.
or

I think Ludmilla grew accustomed to upheaval and treated it as part of the natural order of things.

7. cold fire of the barracuda

Some objects are in their proper place. As Ludmilla grew I saw her face behind the tops of distant trees. Rising above their leafy line like a—what could it be? First her hair, like a bullfighter's cape reflecting itself. Then her forehead, a soft sun that shared its *glow*. And those eyes. Those vivid pools of...glistening sharps? And her nose. Such nose. The cheeks. Soft. But who could tell from such a distance? The mouth. All her beauty could be found in her mouth. Her face rested on that distant outline and looked at me through the window of my flat. I squinted and rubbed my eyes. And then she was here as if she had always been here, cutting my hair, talking about the fragrance of those linden trees that once lined the River Miljacka.

3. the story of alice –

Ludmilla finishes cutting my hair and I sense she is anxious now. She is quiet. I think she is a child and I want to protect her so I tell her the story of Alice.

A young man follows Alice with the intention to steal from her. He follows her to a fancy apartment where she drops off an envelope. The young man breaks into the apartment and finds the envelope. In the envelope he finds a suicide letter signed by Alice. She is going to kill herself. The young man goes home and waits. He waits for hours and then days. He thinks about what to do. He never feels an urgency to do anything until one day he is motivated by some force to look for her. In a few hours he finds out where she lives and when he arrives there he pushes open her door and sees her standing in a large opened window. He is out of breath and lightheaded, but he realizes that he has arrived in time--

I stop because I don't know what I should tell Ludmilla. I don't know how I should finish the story. She looks at me.

'What happens next?' she asks.

Based on all known mathematics of language and semiotic variables, I know there are only two possible endings to the story of Alice:

1.) The young man walks over to Alice and stands in the open window beside her. They look down to the street below. He takes her hand and together they jump, propelled by the force of gravity to an inevitable death.

2.) The young man walks over to Alice and stands in the open window beside her. They look down to the street below. He takes her hand and together they jump, floating off into sky. Below them Sarajevo and the rubble of buildings that will serve as the gravestones of their future deaths.

But I tell Ludmilla a third.

8. goodbye to everyone but me >

The sun sets on the barracuda. The pebbles on the bank of the river are covered then uncovered by water. A cold and simple action that is but the last link of a long, unseen chain.

the world that destroyed the world

the world that destroyed the world

The next to last feeling returned. She had somehow become more and together they looked through the telescope to see the outline of the city. They felt there was no hope here. No sun. No rose that burst forth from a moist cloud. No moonlight that shimmered off the gentle waves of the black river drifting before them. This river. From where they were reborn. From where they emerged and stretched out on the land. On the mud. And left the impression of their coil as proof that they once lived. That they once breathed the same air as they who surrounded their outlines with ribbon. As they who visited at night to lay flowers upon the memory of their disappeared forms. As the snakes and toads that swam in the rain-filled cast of their bodies.

Robert says I should know what it is to have been born as another—running through the spray and spittle of gunpowder, hiding beneath the cart of rotting plums and eggplants. All those other, different faces. All unreal to me through the first light of morning. But Martha, I will call her Martha, whispers around his ill-formed ear that only those who made me could have made me and only at that particular moment in history, and that if not then, then never.

I was an uninvited guest to the gathering. An intruder who was available but unprepared for the diversion. The band in the corner beneath the overarching *taxidermia* of the monstrous neck and head of a giraffe, played in tune (or so it was heard) a particular song that brought Robert and Martha to the checkered floor while others watched around them. I sat quietly and thought *do not think for they can find their way in and even now they have already done so. They have schemed within me to give form to their forged existence.*

I asked the trumpeter if I might have a try for I knew a tune that Martha, as a child, played on the rocks and shells she arranged on the footbridge between the road to the beach and her family home. None were allowed to pass until they covered their ears and waited quietly for her to tap her melody with a stick she hid beneath the handrail of the bridge. But it was I who whittled the stick for her and she thanked me by playing her secret melody early one morning before our families turned in their beds.

Martha did not look up. But Robert watched me. And I watched him. Over the bell, from where the notes blossomed and then died. Maybe she had tapped this song on the balustrade of the staircase they descended together and told him that no one else in the world had ever heard it. How it must have languished in his ear I thought? Each note knocking the corners of that piece of clumsy furniture protruding from his head.

I watched them above the floor—*the lovers*—lingering in the space the other left behind. I could not deny there was a grace in their movements. As if they were of one form, which only separated for the sake of being understood—an imprecise but charming translation. Martha left the room.

'Ladies and gentlemen,' Robert said. 'Martha has gone to pee.'

There was still something left of her old self after all, I thought. Something for me to hold onto. It wasn't all *balcony above the clouds* and the name of electricity firing through. She had many departures, not the least of which the dress of a kingdom falling upon her body. She sat down: *what are we if not living in this world?* The face of a boy from which the trench wail and mask. The year in clips of filth. The coat hanging, the severed arms left in curtain sleeves, shoulder blades and neck scraped away. Martha fled and burst around the spiral.

She saw it all love, belove. She saw it all low, below.

The guests became quiet but it was raining and no one could be certain of what they had heard. Paratrooper John came in with a spoon and champagne balloons, kicking his legs up can-can style to the song playing in his head. We only heard his labored breathing, his 'hups' and 'heys' and we clapped awkwardly to his gasping, the hot breath from his nostrils blowing strands of wet hair from his thick moustache onto the floor. The maids came in and swept up the mess. And then he clenched a fist, raised his arm, and yelled 'The war is over! Hooray!', until he noticed a *moustachito*, black and gleaming, on the floor beneath him.

I accidentally punctured the wall behind me. When I turned around Robert was looking through the window. Beyond him I saw the outline of the city. The rain flowed along the rooftops and spires and surged like a waterfall over the edge of the last building (the truest building), and cascaded down his arm, dripping from the fingers of his hand.

Old Bobby knew the absence would irk me and when he walked away there was so much space beside the city that I fell into a panic. I thought I saw Martha out there in a tungsten ploddy rowing herself to death but she was peeing, although the sound of her peeing was drowned out by drops of rain hitting the oversized pancreatic kettle the gardener kept out back. Robert knocked on the bathroom door but Martha did not answer and when he burst in we saw the open window. Oh the breeze. It blew the curtain out and in and enveloped us with a feeling that most resembled freedom. No one spoke though everyone had ideas about what had happened. I saw them (snarl) just above their heads in perfect spheres that rose up like bubbles and burst upon the ceiling.

I asked Robert if I might cut out my tongue. He nodded and I put my arm around Martha's waist and pulled her close to me. This was *my* Martha. I moved her hair away from her face and pressed my cheek to hers. I watched the back of Robert's head as he walked away, and that ear, the shape of D'Artagnan the elder → hackmate of his Prostruscan master → martyred for a commonly known descriptive phylum → unable to dodge the laments and hoarse cries of *laud me but make no mention*—that ear I could take an ax-mop to, to chop and then mop pieces of into a dust bin and pour into a fire to light anywhere it was too flipping dark to see. The building shook. Robert had climbed the giraffe and straddled the neck like he was hunter Sally.

Meanwhile, my shoulders twitched uncontrollably. I knew the song. It was from our later years and Martha and I moved in perfect accord. As her breasts plunged in, my chest became concave. As my hip thrust forward, her atoms tingled around the striations of my thigh. Bernst called for us as the letters 'endu' from the golden-hewed signage above the front door crackled and hit the ground. But Martha knew no Bernst and followed me as I pulled her here and there. Back across the river to La Republica and cans of mixed vegetables (golden carrots, golden corn, and golden peas), medium-sized chicken eggs and golden-golden dirigibles. I winked for a tango but the music ended and Martha bowed to thank me because she could see that I knew how to boogie. And yet, not a hint of recognition. Not a twinkle in her eye that she had tried to access the deep well of her brain matter to pull me out and bring me front and center. Oh Martha, what is that you cannot see? Someone yelled 'yeeeeehah!'. I heard a bone snap and felt a wobble around my titular array.

When she lived in this place, I held the (blaise) omnibus of our flower.

the drawer of owls

the drawer of owls

It wasn't true that I had killed a policeman as I had no idea of any testament or testimony to such effect. But I wasn't misquoted either when the guava lady told the reporter that she heard me say 'I killed the sweaty son-of-a-bitch dead'. It was the galling hypothesis that I had just come off the boat from Beijing and from a man of authority no less that bristled my sensitive knuckle hairs. I grew ired and reckoned to puff myself up with the intent to aggress upon him all my wares, but I turned away as peacefully as a molly and hitched my shoulders to reason, which had already started running down the road ahead of me. Maybe it looked like I was running away and not after and that's why the recommended authorities gave chase but I figured that if they were giving chase then by all rights and god-given blasphemies I could give unchase.

And I'll admit an odd feeling overcame me as I ran through those dusty and undusty streets. Not so much a feeling as a lack of one because it didn't seem unusual to me to be pressed in such a manner. I felt as if I were walking down the street as calmly as I would on any Thursday afternoon after a few busty grogs of the wink-wink aluminum. I passed the Plaza of Kathmandu where I had drank many a tea and coffee with Maria and then headed across the road to the woods and ran through the trees and bushes until I reached a clearing. On the other side of the clearing stood a building and I thought to make my way across to it but the odd feeling of calm left me and I hesitated, worrying that if the authorities should reach the clearing before I made it across I would be shot in the back. Dead.

But there was nothing else to do and I took off and ran as fast I could. I tried to think about Maria as I ran. About the possibility of never seeing her again. About how this was all her fault. But I kept wondering if I would hear the gunshot or if I would hear nothing. If I would be wounded enough for them to catch up to me and finish me off with another shot. Or if I would realize nothing and be finished off in the middle of a thought without feeling a thing. Would it happen here? Or here? While thinking about the windows of that building or about how tired my legs were becoming?

The shot never came and I reached the building and hid behind a row of hedges that reached up to the first floor windows. From there I had a good view of the clearing and hoped to stay there until dark at which time I intended to steal a car and get out of town. But I saw the police walking in my direction and realized that I couldn't wait it out after all. I stood and turned around to open the window but when I looked in I saw a little boy sitting at a desk looking at me. He turned away and started writing something on a piece of paper. I tried to open the window but it was closed. I tapped on it and the boy looked at me again. I motioned with my hands for him to lift the window but he didn't understand my gesture and he put his head back down. A few moments later he looked up at me and started smiling. He said something but I couldn't hear him. And then he picked up the piece of paper and pressed it against the glass. I saw that it was a picture of an owl. And then he put it back down on the desk and started drawing again. I stood there and waited for him to finish, all the while thinking about whether I should make a run for it. But instead of running I tried to see what he was drawing. I jumped as high as I could but I couldn't jump high enough. The police were still walking across the clearing, pointing to where they thought I was hiding but I waited. And waited. Finally the boy turned to me again and smiled and pressed the piece of paper against the glass and I could see that it was another picture of an owl. Again he said something but I couldn't hear him. And then he looked at me and started crying. A few moments later the door to the room opened. Someone came in and turned on the lights and I saw that the walls of the room were covered with drawings of owls. Owls of different shapes and sizes. Of different colors. From the bottom of the wall to the top. On the ceiling. On the floor. On the door into the room. On all the desks around him. Then he leaned over to the window and drew an owl onto the glass with his finger.

A few moments later, the police found me behind the hedge and walked me back to the clearing. I turned around and saw the boy watching me from the window. I kept turning around to look at him until he was too far away for me to see.

pumice

pumice

'In what intangible way does pumice affect you?'

I had sincere hopes for a resolution to this question on the morning of July 30, 1899 when Mrs. Pomsipomsi brought breakfast to my study. I had fallen asleep on my sofa while going over notes I had written down on General Flow, a theory I championed at speaking engagements at various universities. I had come upon General Flow accidentally while spinning the wheel of a hansom that had fallen on its side when the horse pulling it got loose due to faulty hansom apparatus. Later that day I locked myself in my study and for three months wrote a lengthy article on General Flow that appeared in several respected science magazines distributed throughout the country. Alas, that was many years ago and I have improved upon General Flow, refuting parts of my earlier theory and revising or clarifying other parts. I shall publish the definitive General Flow Theory any day now.

If I remember correctly, on the morning of July 30, 1899 Mrs. Pomsipomsi knocked on my study door and announced she was bringing my breakfast in. I massaged my neck and told her to come in, at which point she entered and rested a tray of boiled egg, buttered toast, salted avocado, and coffee on the desk of cluttered papers and hydrogen tools that I kept as a childish diversion. It was an atavism on my part to have such tools lying around but I felt, as I feel now, that they kept me boisterous.

'Careful with those', I implored her.

But she was always careful and I realized immediately the redundancy of my counsel. She wondered aloud if my neck was troubling me and I responded in the affirmative as to do otherwise would be a prevarication on my part.

'Yes', I remember saying. 'My neck hurts.'

From the street below I heard the adolescent cry of the paperboy rasping out the day's headlines. I made out that P.T.R Crim's daughter had gone missing again, and that the higher courts ultimately dismissed Paulderoy Smithy's charges against the George de Frock Hansom Cab Company, which made me feel self-effacingly nostalgic about the origin of General Flow.

I stood, made my way to the window and opened it to tell the paperboy to throw a paper up to me in exchange for the coin I would throw down to him. As I prepared to catch the day's events, leaning out of the window with my arms spread, I felt a hard slap on my bottom and turned around abruptly with an air of indignation about me.

'What the...?' I started before seeing Mrs. Pomsipomsi with a large, flat book of maps in both hands.

I remember getting the book at one of the university book-sales and would never have imagined it to be used in such a manner and under such peculiar circumstances. Mrs. Pomsipomsi inquired again as to my neck and proceeded to knead, in surprisingly deft fashion, the area around my shoulders. She didn't offer an explanation about the extraordinary occurrence of my bottom slapping so I considered it to be one of those inexplicable human reactions to some perceived unusual stimulus and never mentioned it again. I admit now, as I was reluctant to admit then, that I, in turn, had an inexplicable human reaction to the unusual stimulus of having my bottom slapped.

'Tell me Mrs. Pomsipomsi', I labored to speak under her soothing massage. 'In what intangible way does pumice affect you?'

I had often secretly wondered about the fineness of Mrs. Pomsipomsi's nudity, having never seen her nude before, and the characteristics of her womanly blossom, having come to know and catalogue the diversity and uniqueness of the womanly blossom from over half a lifetime of experiences. However, I, unlike many men of science in my day, respected the sanctity of marriage and dare not provoke or evoke any action that might cause dubiousness about the entirely appropriate and professional relationship that Mrs. Pomsipomsi and I had sustained for so many years. It was no equivocation on my part when I would state to this or that dinner guest that I would be entirely lost without Mrs. Pomsipomsi's loyal and doting service.

Still, the scientific yearning in me, the thirst for knowledge, the base human instinct of curiosity, propelled my thoughts toward a resolution of this mystery. The answer to the pumice question was central to the formation of a hypothesis on any woman's womanly blossom and I felt that with Mrs. Pomsipomsi I was on the verge of pumice. I could have probably told you, however, from my superficial observations, based on her mixed Hungarian and Irish ancestry, the color of her hair, the way she used her hands, the way she walked, the shape of her face, and the way she laughed, the characteristics of her womanly blossom without ever having to see it. And yet…

'I'm not sure I know what pumice is', Mrs. Pomsipomsi said.

I guffawed. I often marvelled at Mrs. Pomsipomsi's lack of education because she carried herself and spoke in a manner entirely consistent with the sophisticated and learned women of those modern times. She had an innate intelligence and I often thought that if only it were stroked, the results would be startling.

I raised my arm to rub my neck and my hand landed beneath Mrs. Pomsipomsi's hand quite accidentally. She continued her massage upon my hand for a few rubs as if she hadn't noticed. As our hands moved in opposite directions I felt a quick jolt of static electricity on my knuckle. She must have felt it too because she stopped and I felt her move slowly back. I turned around to look at her and we looked at each other for a tick before she glanced at that now controversial book of maps that rested on the table beside me. I picked it up and was about to hand it to her when a knock came on the door.

'Paper!' the voice said. 'Your paper sir!'

Mrs. Pomsipomsi cleared her throat.

'I'll get the door', she said.

'Yes, of course', I said. 'Thank you.'

She brought the paper to me and left my study, closing the door slowly behind her. I stared at the book of maps for a moment then ate my breakfast and continued working on General Flow, listening for Mrs. Pomsipomsi's footsteps as she made her way throughout the house.

the elephant peed a lot where the lion died

the elephant peed a lot where the lion died

The elephant peed a lot where the lion died. Wild dogs watched from the bushwork and howled like pickled children. Make that *tickled*.

We shall quietly relive a descent. A famous rock that one known as Jaime LaPinta set foot on millions of years ago is central to our unending search for the beginning of this descent.

Central but unimportant.

The descent began with me thinking about your death. While you were alive. I tried to block the thought of your death by thinking about simple things like electricity or bread but your death was still there. It's a strange thing to think that the human body is so fragile but that a skull can withstand so much. It's an equally strange thing to think that in vice versa.

As each day passed I thought about your death. It came to me at various and unexpected times. While saying hello to a stranger. While deciding what to eat at a local restaurant. While tying my shoelaces.

One day I tried to saw pieces of wood to build things but the saw made me think about your death.

I didn't want to think about your death because the thought was painful to me. Not *ouch* pain, but *help me, I can't go on* pain. Every time we spoke I thought about your death. I thought about how I would feel about your death. I tried not to pretend. I tried to make it real so that I would get as close to the real feeling as I could.

I did it but I didn't want to. I stopped speaking to you. Perhaps you thought you had done something wrong or that I didn't like you anymore. But that's not true. I just couldn't bear to think about your death and see you in front of me at the same time.

Eventually I thought about your death everyday. As soon as I woke up in the morning. When I went to sleep at night. I fought it but no matter how hard I tried, your death was there. It was there on an airplane. It was there crossing the street. It was there sleeping quietly in bed. It was there in your breath. It was there at the lake. On the stairs of the back porch. It was there. It was always there.

'I'm here now too.'

Life life life life life. Sun sun sun. Love love love love love.

'I'm still here.'

I wanted to do something about this thought. This burden. This--

'Overwhelming feeling of meaninglessness that had overcome you.'

Yes. I wanted to do something about it but I never did. Then one day while riding the bus, I realized I started to think about your death in a different way. Shall I say it?

'Yes.'

I love sunny days and the ocean. Baby boy genius. Kisses. The color green. The letter f.

I started hoping for your death. Not really hoping for it, but hoping in a way that would--

'Unburden you from the feeling of meaninglessness that had overcome you.'

Yes. Unburden me from the feeling of meaninglessness etc., etc.. Like it would release me in some way from the meaninglessness etc., etc. I told the bus driver what I was thinking hoping that maybe my thoughts would stick to him and he would drive off with them but he looked at me then pushed me off the bus.

Come back here, I said. I said it so matter-of-factly that I startled myself. I said it in a calm way that made me think about killing him. The bus didn't return but it was an important time in my descent. The fact that those two things happened one after the other only brought the picture into sharper focus for me. Those two things.

The elephant peed a lot where the lion died.

It wouldn't surprise you if I told you that life is not enough. I'm not saying, as they say, that there should be more to life than this. No. I'm saying that life is not enough. I'm saying that there should be more to this than life. And I'm not even talking about an after-life because I don't believe in a before-life. I'm talking about the fucking elephant peeing a lot where the lion died. That's what I'm talking about.

But the half-hoping for your death didn't last very long.

'Don't lie.'

I'm not. But your death was still there. Still creeping around, watching from the bushwork. And before you or anybody else start wondering if it's your death or my death that's talking to me, I'll just tell you that it's just me talking to me. That's just what comes to me when I'm thinking about your death. Maybe it is your death talking. Maybe. But I think it's just me sort of talking to myself. That's what I think. And I'm not representing or symbolizing death or anything. I'm just talking.

When I got home that day after the bus ride I felt like hugging you. At least that's how I felt. But I couldn't. I mean, how could I? Especially since I was half-hoping for your death. No, I couldn't do it. So I just passed quietly by you as you played the piano. I can't remember the song now but I'd like to remember it as something good. Something that I might recognize if I heard it again, something that just happened to be playing on the radio and I'd be able to turn to someone, anyone and tell them that I knew that song.

'Go on.'

No, I don't want to.

'Please.'

No. It's over.

box kite

box kite

I hadn't given up. It just wasn't meant to be. The hippo syndrome I believe. That's what it was called. A two-curtain fait accompli with a written translation below the stage and an applause sign for the symphony. It was la-la land laconic but I didn't fall for it. Oh, they want you to. They want you to know that they have the answers. Systems are bad they write. As if we didn't know. But they show you in a concise, systematic way. Here is what went wrong. Here is what went right. Here is the answer. And they try to keep you in your place with a little praise because in praising you they want you to know that they know what you know and they want you to know that they know what you don't know. Some people listen because they can't tolerate the ambiguity. Others because they need the validation. But I don't listen because h) I don't know my place and f) unlike me, they're full of shit.

I was only passing through anyway. On my way south to one of those places dim with promise. Where a man without a crucible could find one. I'd been talking for a long time. On corners. In parks. In theatres. In stores. On stages. In Cleveland. But no one listens. They like their shit usual.

Two mustards, a bowl of fig, and pasty camel hump to go please.

For example, let's take Brad. They have to know that Brad has sisters. That his mother was raped by his father whom he never knew. That his older brother was killed for being in love with a black girl. That he was molested by his stepfather. That when he was a teenager, he was accused of molesting his cousin. That

117

he has brown hair. That he has brown eyes. That he is right handed. That he is six feet two inches tall. That he talks with an Alabama twang. That despite the south's unsavoury history, his southern culture has relevance. That no matter what happens to him in the 'past' he is capable of redemption in the 'present'. That's Brad. Thank you Brad. You may take your seat beside all the others now.

It's very important for them to know they say because it tells them with whom they are to empathize. But what does it tell us? It tells us that people have become intellectually and emotionally complacent. It tells us that regardless of any radical characterization or plot, the human mind is incapable of thinking beyond the same flimsy skin and limp spine it's grown accustomed to. Greatness is what it always has been. But we know this isn't true. Or so we hope. I had my hopes anyway and I carried them with me to the Foggy Bottom metro stop on my way to Union Station where I planned to hold up signs in protest against dumbness.

Stop being dumb. Dumbness is dumb. I know I'm dumb but I'm not as dumb as you are.

This was the land of redemption, after all. America. People here can be saved from dumbness. It wasn't one of those smaller countries where people were stuck in dumb for the long haul. Through no fault of their own, mind you. But they're put into a box with their own illusions and they live their lives punching shadows in there while the people casting those shadows laugh their asses off.

Did you see her jab? I'm counting my money. I've got a big cheese grater. He almost left a dent.

America is too big for a box. There will always be at least one asshole who figures it out and destroys the illusion for everyone else. Because that's what America is all about. Destroying its own illusions.

It began to rain [Maria stroked my hair] and I took out several items from my bag that I had gathered on my peripateticism. That's a big word and I bet some of you stumble on it. I bet some of you have to look it up. I didn't. I want you to know that I didn't because I'm smart. Because I know the meaning of big words. Because I have a PhD in philosophy and can tell you where Hegel and Schopenhauer diverge, where Kant and Confucius converge, and how an analysis of these verges justifies evil as what is best in man. I can quote Marlowe much less Shakespeare. I draw conclusions from metaphors in the poems of Akhmatova and envisage the future of art. I deconstruct modern man simply by comparing the ebb and flow of history to the contrapuntal constructions in a Bach fugue. I am, in a word, remarkable and that, in turn, gives me the right to tell you what you need to know because you, you my friend, are dumb.

A question arose in the background (like this) as a gadfly and brought the juxtaposition of divergent normals (normalis excommunicatis) into focus. Normal 1 is a function of self-explanation. I, being me, explain myself to me and unintentionally to you. Normal 2 is a function of self-delusion. I, being me, hide myself from me and unintentionally from you. The breaking apart of two agents. A factor of schism 1.

I confess part of me felt pity for Brad. I mean, who wouldn't? That was the purpose of his entire story. At the same time, however, I knew Brad got around and I couldn't help but feel that he was being just a tad selfish. Nevertheless, I was polite to him. I nodded. I gave him a thumbs-up and motioned to him that I had it all under control. I took a deep breath and counted to ten because I didn't want to tell Brad he was dumb. El dummo. Le grand dum dum.

At one, the stream I fell into shaped my awareness.

At two, single matriarchs combined to serenade my bounty.

At three, I gave people frequencies to tune into.

At four, transitions disappeared.

At five, I wrote the question *why?* between my shoulder blades.

At six, hiroshima father breastlespur consumed himself.

At seven, I felt a parade moving around my neck.

At eight, I saw a poster advertising the National Theatre's production of Hedda Gabler, the first woman I ever truly loved. That she was a fiction was beside the point. What was important was that I fell in love with her nobility, her personal vision of the world, her stoic rebellion. The poster distracted me from my protesting and I plotted to find my way into National Theatre to proclaim to Hedda my previous affection for her. That I no longer felt any affection for her was also beside the point. We must make a final accounting of our lives one day and any proclamation to her would be part of that final accounting.

I once imagined that Hedda dreamed of designing great cities in circular patterns with parks and canals and that she and I were a statue in the centre of it all. There was plenty of time to get serious for the sake of our legacy. We were serious, but I mean even more serious: child soldiers, famines, the holocaust, pathogens. Hedda and I stayed on the outskirts of serious. Down by the hem, where there always existed the possibility that we could be cut right off and serious could keep on walking without catching cold.

How has the perception of the golden mean changed in the last two hundred years and was this change in perception a catalyst or consequence of the industrial age?

Then we would run off into the future where she would reassemble and ask me questions that made me pause. What about the suffering of children? Pause. What about overcoming the odds? Pause. What about taking up arms against injustice? Pause. What about renewing hope and fighting destiny? Pause.

And during one of my pauses, she'll take a long walk back to where we started and meet someone named Brad with whom she'll have a revealing conversation by the statue in the centre of our great city. A conversation about ordinary people like grocery clerks and people who work in the service industry and how their lives have as much meaning as the lives of the greatest human beings who have ever lived. About small towns and how they are emotionally, if not demographically, as cosmopolitan as any city in the world. Like Tokyo. That's funny. I know a Brad. Will she really believe him though? He molested his cousin. But she'll tell me he's changed and she'll tell me she's changed and she'll leave a gun on my bedside table in great anticipation because she has a vision of a beautifully ordered world, only to find out later that I died of something common like natural causes just to spite her.

At nine, I heard feeble complaints about being condescending.

At ten, I wondered what they were looking at. I watched their dumb eyes. They leaned down over me. All that time I thought they were following my hand as I pointed to their dumbness. I felt the sun shine on my jugular even as the rain fell around me. A gust of wind blew around my hair and a kite rose up from my neck. I felt a pull on my skin. It was me and I ascended until I vanished through the clouds. I thought I'd finally get my answer to the only question. I felt a scribbling on my back and when it stopped, I turned my head until I saw me coming back through the clouds. I pulled but I was too eager. The string snapped and I disappeared from my view. And I thought, well yes, it wasn't meant to be. For who deserves an answer to the only question?

But someone—one of those dummies said: look at what's on your back.

And I said: what?

And he said: I don't know.

Just like a dummy I thought.

Maria, take us out of here.

contratone

contratone

Egad, the handwoven bon-bon triumphs yet again. Like a flintblock of paper ink, a dual free assembly. Musicians, pipers, graters, lovely table cloths, and corn-free fields of roaming. Jeller opposes, recants, supposes, and remarks: 'what strife upon my living, ere upon my strife thus strafe'. I thought it nonsense and being an Englishman threw pastels of soft and girly hues upon him.

the letter m

the letter m

there is no letter m anymore

there is only the letter a

(Oh gentle rain.)

The city is filled with tourists who flitter from place to place, snapping pictures, behaving like outsiders in their own country. And though they aren't outsiders, they don't belong here either. They dress funny. They walk funny. They sit with their legs open and yell because they don't know nuance, as if they wish to overpower the 'foreignness' of this place with their homegrown homilies and late night television banality. But nobody here's laughing.

'How beautiful' they'll say then go home and tell their neighbors (neighbor lovey-dovey) how the people were cold and high falootin' when it was only the fact that they themselves weren't up to the task.

Jeller meets his strife here. Juniper and Jeller. Two cosmonauts strumping the galaxy, tiptoeing upon the ear of governance to whisper a boom the likes of which Robert himself could hardly imagine. Cursed and thirsty, the limpies mock the arm, the leg, and (most distastefully) the bosom.

Meanwhile Nester flints his traction, lamenting that his destiny had found a new vessel. Lamenting that where he sought finality he found only conclusions.

Conclusion #1: *The letter j*

Such statements, provocative to the intellect, fester like a babby's nose in a beautifully constructed pram of delicious orbit. The wheels just so. The soft, white blanket glowing all around. Let us push it 'among the stars'. And though against the backdrop of the universe we appear to move in place, Robert assures us we move not in vain. The old men called Twinkles deliver disagreement. The boon. The supple waif of a tingle and pictures of marble, shaped like ruin suggest the hand of a faithless chiseler.

External. Internal. Pro and pend. Post and send...

The secret pulsates in the body of children until (l)imitation snuffles it out. So what is man? A child % lost # in a f^^orest of ** sym!bols? Ŧ. Nothing could be more untrue. For a man is a man. Not a child. Not as brave. Not as imperv-v-v. Not as impervlav-v-v-b. *Motherfucker.* Not as impervious.

The

letter

u.

Conclusior #2: *unhinged fish scales float to the surface and shimmer in light*

(My breath is of the panther.)

These symbols represent a sense of beingness. A clutter of happening and happenstance that would not be possible without them (these symbols). Strange Jeller. Hinge Jeller. Strange. Hinge. Jeller. And upon the surface they do shimmer. Messages are reproduced and glistening for a moment upon the lips of man, licked off by a fat, juicy tongue. Lick them so in time before the pain of absence.

I being Madeiran shine a light of bright and purple purple upon it to reveal that the scene of beingness, the existential situation (om du vill) collapses at the first wave of the arm to leave us with nothing but air to juggle. No. Not air. Frair. Nester flints his traction again. And lo, clever Juniper, traveling from dumpster to dumpster to find furniture for the modest flat, builds herself quite the empire.

The letter s.

Conclusion #3: *in love with other songs, the notes leave their measure*

And so it is with Juniper and Jeller.

Yes I'm am.

And yes, you're am too.

we are the dogs

we are the dogs

He was sleeping when someone or someones broke into his apartment and stole his television. He complained to the building custodian who told him to stop using the stairs because the children of very important people who lived on the seventh floor played at the bottom of those stairs with little metal cars they had gotten as a Christmas gift from diplomats at the nearby Embassy of Burkina Faso. The building custodian said the children parked their little metal cars beneath the last step so if he happened to come down the stairs in a rush and didn't see the little metal cars he might crush one of them with his (what are those?) size 9 shoes and 'isn't that worse than sleeping'? But he couldn't sleep. All that night he heard dogs barking. Crooning. The gruff metabolizing into some kind of pudding ball splatting against the inside walls of his head. He gave the custodian a 'tsk tsk' and dismissed him with the flick of his veritable wrist.

As he walked out the door, he spied the discount bazaar and part-time concert hall where he and his fondle mate Justine (with cheeks of Indian corn) saw The Mittens perform and where he bought a scarf because of the depressing forecast of a 'long, cold winter' announced by the TV weatherman while he ate his noodles and drank his water and waited for the announcement of the winning Super Megaball numbers. It was the first time he played the Super Megaball and he hit three of the seven numbers and although three of the seven numbers wasn't good enough to win, he thought 'I hit three of the seven numbers'. He told his father, who never thought he was good with numbers, and showed him the Super Megaball ticket as proof.

On his way to the bazaar he popped into the liquor store where he bought his cigarettes. As he walked he remembered that the last images he saw before he fell asleep were from a commercial about a dishwashing rinse-aid that left dishes unstained and sparkling. He thought maybe his apartment needed a plant. The air was humid. The laundro-mat he passed was busy and since they installed a television in one of the upper corners of the room they had been busier than ever. No one could hear what the actors were saying over the grinding of washing machines and dryers but the subtitles were on so people heard the voices in their heads. He thought that was clever. A good way of getting people to clean their shirts and pants. But the fan had gone missing without explanation. People wanted to ask about the fan but as far as he could tell no one ever did. It was 'an' mystery.

On his way to Lorenzo's someone said 'hi' and he said 'hey'. He rarely said 'hello' or even 'howdy'. Those greetings were too formal and led to more formal conversation. He wasn't prone to long-winded monologue about this, that, or the other and often summed up events in just that manner: 'Yes, this, that, or the other happened and here I am.' People who met him thought he was unfinished, as if his being had been colored outside his lines.

But Justine was line blind. She saw only color. She had said 'hey' to him one day and that was enough to water the seed of a soon to be flowering plant. Not long after they met she'd go over to his place and they'd watch television. Yesterday, after he took three busses and walked two miles to pay his electric bill lest his only power go out, he and Justine watched a documentary about perfume. It made him search his apartment for any cologne or scent he might have but he didn't find any. After Justine went home, he fell asleep on the couch. When he woke up it was darker than ever. It was as if the world had come to an end but it was only that someone had moved him from his couch to the closet. It was a hollow feeling because it made him realize that sometimes when you think the world is coming to an end it really isn't.

There was only one shoe in the closet and he thought he was lucky to be sleeping on it. When he opened the closet door, he saw the door to his apartment was opened and his television was gone. It was like a blank space on a test and nothing to fill it in with. Just a lack of knowledge. A panic that he hadn't studied came over him. He closed the closet door so he wouldn't see what wasn't out there. *The fucking rinse-aid* he thought. That could have been the last image he would ever live to see. He vowed never again to fall asleep during a commercial break. *As long as I fucking live.*

But he figured he'd just be frank with Justine. Tell her exactly what happened. His television was stolen. It was as simple as that. What she would do at that point was up to her. She was a grown woman and could do whatever she wanted to do. He decided it was a basic equation. Tell her something and then she could do something or not do something, which in a way was the same thing as doing something. So he could tell her something and then she could do something. It was all up to her. He called her on a payphone and told her about his television but instead of stopping there he went on to tell her about the rinse-aid. She asked him if he was sure that was the last image he saw before he fell asleep; if maybe he didn't have a dream he couldn't remember that might have offered a more poetic image. But it wasn't a good argument he said because at any point, maybe just after he fell asleep—she said 'you're right' before he finished his sentence and asked him what they were going to do that night. He told her maybe they could do their laundry. Justine was silent. It was as if he had said something he shouldn't have said. He told her that he had a garbage bag that she could put her laundry into while he waited outside. She said that wasn't necessary as she had a garbage bag of her own. But she said she didn't want to do her laundry. They had a television there he said but she said she didn't want to hear the voices in her head. She wanted to hear the voices of the actual people saying words. She said she'd give him a call in a couple of days after she got things sorted out.

It was a disagreeable conversation and it uncovered a feeling of despair he had been trying to hide from himself that day. He could have been dead and no one would have known. He thought it was okay to think no one would have known because if the thieves did kill him they would have closed his door. But his absence wouldn't have made too much difference. Sure, he would be remembered but being remembered wasn't the same as being alive. The next day people would be stuck in the same traffic, feel the same heat, inhale the same exhaust. Or they would look out into a field of grass somewhere and breathe in that sweet air and feel the sun or breeze or maybe both on their skin.

He told his brother about what happened and his brother reminded him that the apartment door was left open and that by leaving the apartment door open the thieves had also robbed him of any real insight to be gleaned from the incident. The incident? He couldn't figure out what difference that made but his brother said that what he was having was just pseudo-insight because he was really in pseudo-danger. His brother said he was the victim of a double-entendre and asked him for the Phillips screwdriver. His brother just couldn't believe him when he said it was the worst thing that had ever happened to him. And all that stuff about how Justine had to get things 'sorted out'? His brother said that wasn't enough. And besides, did he really want to go down that insight road? It becomes addictive. One insight every once in a while isn't enough. You start looking for one every week, then every day, and before you know it you're some kind of insight junkie living what seems to be a meaningful life but is as meaningless as if you've never had an insight in your life.

Yeah, well, he had to go. He'd catch his brother later. He shouldn't have stopped by he thought. His brother always made him feel a little bit less and it usually took him a day and a half to recover. Without Justine around it might take even longer.

He could handle the whole job thing not working out. But his television? And then Justine? He decided without self-pity that he was a failure and that he wanted Justine to be his last failure. If only failure was a disease that if went untreated caused death. At least then he could die from something. But he had to go on living. He remembered he was sick in school once. He passed out in gym class and when he came to he was lying on a cot in the nurse's office and this girl named Vanessa who he'd always been interested in was sleeping on a cot beside him. He thought that might be the start of something between them. A shared sickness. He would just lie there until she woke up and then pretend that he was waking up too and then their eyes would meet accidentally and he would smile ever so slightly to show her that he understood her plight. But the nurse saw that he was awake and told him that someone else was sick (who else but Arturo?) and that since he was awake and feeling better that he should leave. He put on his shoes and left, taking one last peek at Vanessa before the nurse closed the door behind him.

The memory reminded him of Justine, who he only saw yesterday, but suddenly felt enough distance from to be reminded of. A few days ago when they were at Lorenzo's together, he looked at her through one of those striped plastic straws Lorenzo's was famous for. She was sitting right across the table from him but through the straw she seemed so far away. And alone. All by herself even though the deli was crowded. It seemed like there was no noise in her little straw world either. That must have meant something he thought. At the time it was just something he did but thinking back on it now it seemed like a meaningful incident. Maybe if he had kept the straw he could have looked through it anytime he wanted to and see Justine in there. His strawbaby. He wrote that down so he could tell his brother the next time he saw him. He taped the note to his fridge so he could see it every day and not forget it. But he had to remember to take it down if he ever invited his brother over or if his brother came to visit unannounced.

He still liked his brother but his brother didn't know everything about him. There was the time he stepped on a hypodermic needle in the parking lot of the Sixteenth Street Baptist Church and ran home scared because he thought he saw tracks pushing up through the skin on his arm. That memory festered in his spirit for years. Or the time when he liked—well, the whole Vanessa incident. What a great rift in his soul that created. Then he tried to work himself up into some kind of misery: *I could have been dead. Oh Vanessa* (he meant Justine). But it didn't work and then he realized his brother was right. He reached out to the television but it wasn't there. It had become a habit and he decided that he either had to get a new television or stop trying to turn it on.

The next day his parents visited and asked him if he had ever been to Paris because they were interested in going. He had to think about it. He almost lied and told them yes. Sometimes he did that.

phonoplane

phonoplane

People want to be happy and control the future. There are no tyrants here. An approximate cross-pollination might suffice in this regard. Further. Was what was. Further.

Under the luau, the majus pristine, blanched by invisible particles and the timely life of my pedigree. Brrrrojo [restore] amarino [untie] azun [restore]. The difference between getting and the phonoplane. The difference between sleeping and the drier parts of stone. These things matter. You may find your way down the hill, after all.

At bottom a camel is human in so far as it is not spoken of first. We spoke of camels midstream and contemplated their bundle. An ancillary effect compensated for by our disdain for desert spittle.

The boy and his train. A faint bell stop unsummoned.

I knew it was all about him. This telling. To come so close to the understanding that he breathes finer air than I and not to breathe it. But who could take such a thing from him? I carried his door-like plastic. Then he. And lay him on the blanket. Cornered west and straddled to find way of the girl (the girl). Freda. Whose hair covers his sleep. Who makes space in the morning for the sun to admire his face.

I want to tell you something about the boy Freda. Follow me to the meadow. And she did and the boy who came running out with sword and calling for me.

Just to see. Those block-line filaments. The three [two] parts of sundry.

'It's time to go', she says.

But before I move we sit and look through the window. Maybe the frank (I think it plain). Maybe the dauphin: *in minor centuries.*

I am of the mind to leave her and let her find her own way.

'It's time to go', she says.

Like the time one made mention of greater things— first drop and penchant—I put him on his bicycle and sent him down the hill—unexpected ascension (a far point astray). I'll pick him up. I'll get him. Bring him from the station. Have a dance—and should an eyelid come undone—

Let me tell you about the boy Freda.

It's not easy to build a tree but I have gathered leaves for the pasting. Watch us from the balcony and feed on our gaze.

'I had a dream that normal friend-like budlings fell on my face and between them I saw the boy standing on a bare limb looking down on me.'

Up there he seems smaller.

Connection [brings one greatness].

Connection [keeps one from becoming more].

An element of physiology. Stur. It will be all that is left when we are gone. The dream, sweetful and more famous than air, a thank you and good-bye. We may draw colors and swing free the hand and hammer but if the rain stops today and we sit shoulder to shoulder. She said my son. She said the camel. There are Romans here and the names of Romans.

Let me tell you about the boy Freda. I'll whisper so no one else can hear. Slowly.

The boy will love you.

X postulate.

Chromosome decelerator.

The phonoplane.

But then again, he may not.

love letters from satan

love letters from satan

Letter 1:

Dear Friend,

It would have been better for me if I had been a dairy farmer instead of Satan but my selflessness was ingrained in me at an early age. How could I allow another to suffer the humiliation and ostracism I have suffered? You might think it difficult for me to find a pleasant little nook to settle into but I have found a small room to live in above a tobacco shop across from the University Hospital where I was born Tundey Abikinabi. You would be surprised to know that despite my lack of formal education or military training I still manage to pay the two-hundred and fifty dollars rent each month, which conveniently enough, includes all the washing of my dirty linens and a once a month shining of the old boots worn by my father.

I apologize I could not meet with you last week but I did hear the news that Roger Spato insulted you while at the theatre. Don't worry my friend. I assure you that I am Roger Spato. I am also Spato's wife Penelope as well as Lilibeth, their darling daughter. I write letters to her of a startling clarity. I can send a copy of one to you if you like for I make copies of all my letters, including this one. It is, with all humility, an endeavor of a historical nature.

I write to tell you that I bring the world a new way. Or rather a new perspective of an old and calamitous philosophy. By the way, if while reading this letter you happen to hear music, do not be surprised. Twice a week, a quartet plays outside my window and they arrive punctually and in tune. At the moment, they are applying themselves to a vivacious adaptation of a Janacek concerto.

Speaking of beasts, dear friend, the grocery store is not far and I would like to invite you for a little bite of supper one of these good nights. I am on very good footing with the grocers and I doubly assure you that they put aside all the best legumes for me. Is it not bizarre how France, Germany, and England are claimed to be the fashionable legume countries now when everyone knows the best legumes are to be found here? Imagine my surprise when I picked up the newspaper this morning to read of this. It is such a tedious endeavor to appease the Europeans but appease them I shall. Only in the French language is it even possible to subscribe to such flighty notions so I will assume they were the ring leaders of this malfeasance.

As to our supper and my explanation of the new way, I urge you to accept my generous invitation. We are both free men, unencumbered by career or family concerns and one night away from all the mind-numbing festivities of this time of year might do you well. Do not be troubled that only I will be speaking. You will certainly have events to relate to me as it pertains to the new opera I am writing. You did hear did you not? A liberating account of the dog races played out on a bifurcated stage where the upper half represents—what else?—heaven, and the lower half, my little room. Wear panties. The new way is rather warm.

Love always,
Satan

Letter 2:

Dear me, an altogether sacred friend, you,

Last we met, I had the divine misgiving to announce that the King of Liechtenstein, his Royal Highness Abner, was to be shot before me during the Festival of Burt. Allow me to inform you now that the announcement was premature. In as much as Abner, the son of Jesus Christ and Ruth, is best served unshot, we will have his head in good time. This is a fortuitous circumstance because I would like to give you, dear friend, the pleasure of making the future announcement with the headline to read: ABNER GRAVEL HEAD.

I feel terrible that our supper progressed so rapidly. For our next meeting, a long, untangled feast will be served, should I have the wherewithal to employ the riding cockles. I confess I was rushed as I am in the habit of having what I want when I want without much consideration for those around me. In the future, I will try to be more considerate.

I am writing this same letter to Our Lady of Good Standing, Philomena, in which I will replace her name for yours. It is an intractable habit of mine and I ask you to forgive me. Do you find it odd to hear me speak of forgiveness? I studied forgiveness in primary school under the stern tutelage of my father.

When I spoke to you of the vesper, I had the royal butcher on my mind. An understandable distraction completely beyond my control. There is something of an oiling taking place at Harold House and the royal butcher, that mongrel savant, plays more of the pomade than the filly pot. Do not think it terrible of me to speak out of turn, for sensible beings in insensible places are ultimately profound in their gossip. As to your observations on my opera, I cannot entirely disagree with you. However, you must certainly see the wisdom of having the character Zarathustra perfumed with the musky aroma of crusade.

I am currently recreating the world, music notwithstanding, in the image of a prat. All my deeds—I can hardly say good and bad—will coalesce there and, in time, disperse as the River Sophocles. I am John the Baptist. I anoint you Saladin.

With Love,
Satan

Letter 3:

Dear Petronius Flavius, mullah of Akbar province,

I write to your alias because I am cross with you.

How little they think of me Petronius? And you too. Even you my friend denied me as the cuckoo clock cuckooed the hour of seven at the Festival of Burt. So allow me to address you with a more sinister tone.

My name should well be synonymous with man's highest achievements. Wherever you have seen man perform great deeds, never forget that it is your friend who did this. It is all well and good to daydream in a fruity garden and smack one's soft, tender lips to the juices of fruitiness—

I confess that I stopped writing at this point to answer my door. The rest of my thought continues below.

But to dare, to will, to overcome? For what is life without these instincts that without me would not have existed? These were my gifts to man and I gave them unconditionally. I do not think it too much to ask, however, that I be shown the smallest gesture of gratitude. Must I demonstrate how gratitude can be empowering?

Again, I confess I was interrupted due to my having to explain the operation of a new flushing mechanism. My thoughts continue below. I am grateful for your patience.

Instead, my name is blighted as if I were some braggadocio wooing the wife of my good friend Napoleon, whose arsenal I gifted with my rather large genius. Perhaps I am to blame. I was angry when I inspired man to turn my father's work into religion. For now, ironically, religion has turned against me despite my tithing to its cause. But good parenting is not playing favorites. A child notices such behavior and as children themselves, I thought man was created with the intelligence to understand this.

I shall write a poem to absorb this hurt I feel and allow you, as a gesture of renewed love, to find it among your bric-a-brac as a Shakespeare sonnet.

When I was Shakespeare, I felt a kinship with man I had not felt before or since that time.

Of all the wonders that I yet have heard, it seems to me most strange that men should fear; seeing that death—

Oh, it's all quite a bore now isn't it?

I have an appointment on Thursday next with a Dr. Heron. A dentist whose specialty is the treating of inflamed molars. Would it be presumptuous of me to ask that you go with me? I tried in vain to persuade the good doctor that my molars are in their normal state but he would hear none of it and insists on surgery. I believe the bird wants to insert my teeth into his niece.

If only I could write more but I hear the pope finishing in the toilet and he wishes to speak to me on some urgent matter. I had a new toilet installed in advance of his visit and it cost me a considerable portion of my salary. I would like you to see it and give me your thoughts.

I will place this letter in an envelope and have the pope mail it for me when he leaves. I hope it reaches you in good health.

I am no longer cross with you.

With love,
Satan

Letter 4:

Dear friend whom I now call Mahatma,

You will not be surprised to read that I know a thing or two about curiosity and I understand completely your desire to read one or two of the letters I have written to Lilibeth. Do not feel ashamed if I have caught you off guard but I did hear of the aforementioned desire at the

Boodlestein's Troupe rehearsal of my new opera 'Dog the Mutton'. In this envelope, you will find one of those letters, which in the interest of posterity I call *The Lilibeth Letters*, for your perusal.

It begins vapidly enough Dear Lilibeth, and continues with all of the usual flourishes consistent with the fashion.

Notice however, between those flourishes of convention a keen awareness of Lilibeth's situation as a young, untouched daughter of rather Presbyterian parents. It is a repugnant situation I assure you and if I cannot pry the girl away from their sordid preaching with my own hands, I will endeavor to do so with those same hands vicariously.

Yes, laugh my friend laugh. I think you are laughing but if you are not do not think of my statement as a command. The enclosed letter, written under the guise of one Rupert the Harpsichordist, began the great coitus of words between Lilibeth and me. She writes remarkably well for a high priestess but she does have a tendency to compromise her labial phonemes. I have tried in subtle ways to correct her of this habit but to no avail.

You have caught me in a good mood Mahatma. The opera rehearsal. The meeting with the pope. He is a decent fellow but if you have him for dinner I want to tell you that I believe he suffers from an affliction of the most unfortunate variety. But he came to me well recommended by the owner of the tobacco shop who himself is a ghastly plebe but extremely likable and to whom I promised the favor of a meeting. As for the money I owe you, do not believe I have forgotten. I have taken a second job in the evenings working at a bookshop and will put off the purchase of a new iron until I have repaid my debt to you. If, however, you are obliged to take my father's boots as collateral until that time I have saved enough money for both the iron and repayment of my debt to you, I will appear for our next supper with a very pronounced pleat indeed.

With Love,
Satan

Letter 5:

Dear Placenta,

I am not in the mood to write to you tonight but something occurred today I would like you to know about. Lilibeth Spato visited the bookshop. She browsed for quite a long time before she purchased a copy of The Man Who Was Thursday. She looked at me, knowingly as is said in some circles, and said hello. Perhaps she noticed the number of fingers I have. It would have been enough to give me away. I could not be certain and as I walked home, I replayed her eye movements in my head and concluded she did not notice.

Still, I have resolved to be more careful and since her visit to the bookshop, I have resorted to wearing mittens in public.

I have also been busy with mathematics. I have calculated the amount of free time I have each day and I realize that it is far too much for someone like me to be idle. However, with this free time, I have deigned to do something constructive and have created a new calendar and new terminology for the telling of time. Oddly enough, my new calculations based on these new paradigms suggest I do not have much free time at all, which suits me perfectly. When I did have free time, I was overly reflective, as you may have noticed during our last conversation.

I was not bold enough to say it then but you are fortunate to have known your mother. Imagine my life without a mother to comfort me when I fell. Without a mother to cuddle with when daddy turned his attention elsewhere as he often did. Without even a photograph or memory to look upon on those cold, winter nights and feel warm and cozy. I lament that ours was not the ideal family, but as I have very little free time now, I shall have very little time in which to lament.

Oh happy day.

I have three tickets to The Punky Plays. I came close to imposing on Lilibeth the favor of attending with me since I am her father but I have decided to invite you and a woman I met at the bookstore by the name of Donatien, who coincidentally has my eyes. She and I engaged in an enlightened conversation on the qualifications of young women in the staging of Punky One and Punky Two, of which she was most knowledgeable. She is very young and I implore you to get to know her as I will make something memorable of her one day. Be mindful, however, that she has not seen Punky Three and I would like her, as I desire with all youth, to experience the new sensations with the un-jaded enthusiasm of the innocent.

By the way, I touched Mary last night. It will not make you happy but I cannot tell a lie. And as I do not have a mother to blame, and as I do not believe in blame, what of it? Believe me when I say that there is no one more true to his and her own self than I.

Alas, last night combined with the events of today have made me uncharacteristically sleepy. That is all the free time I have, and will not be able to write to you again, unless my calculations are incorrect and I have more.

Forever yours,
Satan

www.ingramcontent.com/pod-product-compliance
Lightning Source LLC
Chambersburg PA
CBHW032013170626

46807CB00006B/2786